# Chief Seattle
# Man of Vision

## By

## Florence Westover Bond

## Cover graphic by Carl E. Bond

ISBN: 0-75965-085-3

This book is printed on acid free paper.

1stBooks - rev. 8/6/01

# Synopsis

This biography of the famous Native American traces his life and the development of the Puget Sound region and how each affected the other.

The book sets the stage by describing the lifestyle of the Indians on the Whulge (Puget Sound) and the early encounter Seattle had with the English Captain George Vancouver.

As Seattle grows to manhood, he finds his guardian spirit, the spirit of peace, his tribe begins to construct a great home-fortress, Tsu-Suc-Cub, and Seattle begins to dominate the life of his tribe.

Through a series of events with enemy tribes to the east and north, Seattle becomes the most powerful chief on the Whulge.

Increasing white migration begins to affect life on the Whulge. Seattle works to help his people adapt to the resulting changes.

Ultimately, Seattle makes a decision, which carries profound implications: he decides to keep the Whulge part of the United States.

As time takes its toll on Seattle, he endears himself to white and Indian alike; he then slowly slips away.

This biography, intended for young adult and adult readers, gives the famous Native American an authentic human character with all the attendant strengths and weaknesses that individual possessed. This book would be appropriate for Washington State history courses, which are required by many colleges and school districts in the state. There is increasing interest in the Puget Sound region as the importance of that region to world markets and the volatile world economy increases. This book places a human quality on the early days of the region; the book is an excellent place for a study of Puget Sound to start. It is also interesting to remember that the famous chief was born just over 200 years ago, a short length of time for such profound changes as shown herein.

Although many reference books give one or two page summaries of Chief Seattle's life, there are no biographies of him in print. Those summaries tend to largely agree with the story line in this biography. In fact, for a person who had such a profound effect on U.S. and world history, there is precious little available at this time.

# For

# Denny

# Editor's Note

This book is a biography of a Native American leader whom we shall call Seattle. The spelling of his name is in dispute for two reasons. First, his name is an English translation from the Duwamish dialect. That translation is subject to interpretation. Second, Seattle may have thought it bad luck to have one's name spelled correctly on one's headstone. "Sealth" is on the headstone. If it were spelled correctly, it may be bad luck. As you will see in the book, Seattle was a gambler, therefore luck was no doubt a big concern.

This book contains extensive dialogue between historical figures. It is impossible to verify the accuracy of this dialogue. However the author, my paternal grandmother, had important contact with some of these people. She wrote the entire text prior to 1970. I have therefore, worked to leave that material untouched as much as possible. I believe this book provides an overall accurate representation of the period it describes and of the life of a great American.

This book also documents the concept that Chief Seattle made the conscious and deliberate decision to maintain the Whulge (Puget Sound) Basin as part of the United States. As a result, he remains a towering figure of United States and world history. His influence will extend well into the Third Millennium.

Nick Bond
Olympia, Washington
February, 2000

# Chapter Outline

Chapter One; Indians on the Whulge: The setting of the book is described, the Whulge (Puget Sound) with its mild climate and plentiful resources; the Indians native to the area, some of their customs and their way of life. The child Seattle is born. The tribe chooses a nomadic lifestyle for the summer of Seattle's seventh year. 910 words.

Chapter Two; A Phantom Appears: While on their camping trip, Seattle's tribe spots the ship (phantom) of Capt. Vancouver exploring the Whulge. Seattle's tribe assists the expedition. The plans for Tsu-Suc-Cub (Seattle's home for the rest of his life) are conceived. 1339 words.

Chapter Three; A Luminous Sea Gull: At fourteen, Seattle sets off to find his guardian spirit, the spirit of peace. Thus the tone for Seattle's adult life is set. 756 words.

Chapter Four; Tsu-Suc-Cub: A tribal fortress-home is built, after some dispute. Seattle begins to dominate the life and leadership of his tribe. The massive scope of Tsu-Suc-Cub is described. 1086 words.

Chapter Five; Thunderbirds: Seattle's tribe is attacked by Indians from the north, Seattle begins to unite the Indians of the Whulge into a single force. 1950 words.

Chapter Six; A Bold Adventure: Another provocation from the north brings a counter attack from the Indians of the Whulge. As Seattle continues to increase his leadership, he experiences first-hand the horrors of war. Victorious in battle, Seattle follows the enemy north and lays waste to their abandoned homes. 2226 words.

attends. The boundary between the U.S. and Canada is established. 2419 words.

Chapter Fourteen; Visions of the White Man: The advance of settlers continues overland, while Seattle and Leschi observe and comment. Tumwater and Olympia are established. Leschi assists settlers. Seattle and Leschi participate in the changes brought about by the white migration. 2684 words.

Chapter Fifteen; The White Medicine Man: Seattle welcomes the settlers who will found the town which now bears his name. Whites benefit from Indian assistance. Some cultural differences appear. Seattle learns of the arrival of Dr. Maynard in Olympia. Seattle and Maynard develop a friendship. Seattle moves Maynard north. 2212 words.

Chapter Sixteen; Metropolis of the Northwest: Maynard participates in the platting of a new town. After some discussion, the name for the town is chosen: Seattle. 1091 words.

Chapter Seventeen; A New Trail: Leschi assists in making Tumwater the new terminus for the Oregon Trail. The settlers overcome hardships as they meet with success. 1263 words.

Chapter Eighteen; Treaties: The ambitions of the whites, especially the new territorial governor, conflict with Indian ownership, especially Leschi's. The governor rethinks his position and negotiates a second treaty. Seattle delivers his speech. New treaties are signed, old promises are repeated. 3766 words.

Chapter Nineteen; Port Madison Reservation: Tensions rise as implications of treaties and unkept promises are realized. Under Seattle's leadership, and with his youngest daughter,

Princess Angeline's help, the Duwamish tribe is successfully relocated. 2265 words.

Chapter Twenty; War Clouds: Background for Indian complaints further explored. Leschi becomes increasingly involved in action against whites as Seattle continues to support them. Seattle and Leschi in head to head discussion. Leschi leaves beloved farm for the last time. Indians and whites each prepare for conflict. Seattle moves closer to making the most important decision of his life. 3165 words.

Chapter Twenty-One; The Battle of Seattle: Provocations send Leschi and whites on collision course. Seattle takes steps to prevent or lessen effects of conflict. Seattle decides to keep the Whulge (Puget Sound) as part of the United States. Leschi retreats. Reward of fifty blankets offered for Leschi's capture. 2930 words.

Chapter Twenty-Two; Trial for Murder: Leschi tried for murder on trumped up charges. Seattle and others try to get Leschi off. Leschi executed. Seattle and Maynard mourn Leschi. 1352 words.

Chapter Twenty-Three; Peace at Last: Seattle and Maynard wrestle with bureaucracy and reminisce about past mistakes and explore future opportunities. Seattle's health worsens. Seattle crosses the Whulge one last time to visit Princess Angeline and the newly constructed building for the University of Washington. Slowly, Seattle slips away. 2051 words.

Biographical Sketch: The life and background of the author. 412 word.

Book Length: 41, 659 words

# Contents

# Chapter One

## Indians on the Whulge

The Indians of the Pacific northwest were fortunate, for nature provided them with the necessities. Herds of elk and deer roamed the vast forests eating tender sprouts and green leaves. Black bear that hibernated in hollow logs and hollow stumps came from their hiding places in the early spring to devour the buds and berries that grew beneath the trees. Ducks, geese, and other migratory birds made good targets for the arrows of Indian hunters.

Lakes and streams were alive with trout. Beaches along the sea burst with clams and oysters. Inasmuch as the Indians had large seagoing canoes, the Pacific Ocean supplied them with unlimited quantities of seafood—everything from whales and sea otters to smelt and crabs.

Vegetation grew abundantly in the rich river valleys and on the foothills of mountains. Indian women and children gathered the edible roots and greens. They picked crabapples, strawberries, blackberries, raspberries, and salmon berries in the early spring. In the fall, they gathered blueberries, huckleberries, and salal berries. Much of the food they gathered was dried or smoked and stored for winter consumption.

Warm ocean currents moderated the climate west of the Cascade Mountains. The Indians smeared their bodies with whale oil, so little clothing was needed. Such garments as were worn were fashioned from skins of animals or from cloth woven from dog hair, feathers, and cedar bark.

Storms that came from the Pacific Ocean sent huge quantities of driftwood onto beaches. These piles of driftwood furnished firewood and material for the houses built along the shores.

Some Indians erected their houses on hillsides above the beaches. Huge hand-hewn cedar planks were used to construct the buildings. Some of the villages had potlatch houses. The families and slaves of the chiefs and other leaders usually occupied these houses. The potlatch houses had no windows and one door. The pillars of the houses were ornamented with figures representing guardian spirits and the legends of the occupants. Hanging mats from the ceiling made compartments inside the buildings.

Two platforms were built along the walls, one above the other. The top ones were covered with mats and furs. The chiefs and family members slept there. The lower ones were used for seats during the day. At night they became the sleeping places of the slaves.

Fishing and hunting equipment, watertight baskets, and other household supplies were stored beneath the lower platform. Furs, dried clams, smoked fish, roots, and dried berries were kept in bins above the upper platform.

The Whulge, so named by the Indians, was a large inland body of water that joined the Strait of Juan de Fuca. On its shores dwelt the powerful Duwamish tribe. On the opposite shore, lived the Suquamish Indians. Their chief, Schweabe, as an ambitious young brave, would look across the water and imagine that some day he'd become chief of all the Indians on both sides of the Whulge.

Schweabe took for a bride a beautiful Duwamish maiden. Their son, Seattle, was born in the spring of 1786. The tribe was camped on an island picking berries when the baby arrived. Fishermen went out in canoes to catch salmon, which were roasted on hot rocks. Hunters entered the woods in search of game. Dried berries and roots were cooked in watertight baskets. There was hiyu muckamuck for all.

Chief Schweabe and the war chief, Kitsap, like most of the braves of the tribe lived out-of-doors much of the time, either in the forest or on the ocean. But in winter, when mist covered the mountains or storms blew in from the ocean, the braves stayed indoors to keep out of the rain even though the homes were filled to overflowing with people and dogs.

The men of the tribe sat around campfires to powwow while women and slaves did the work. Warriors told tales of bravery and endurance, of atrocities, of the glories won in war. Often Seattle slipped into his house, sat close to his father, and listened to all that was said. He admired Kitsap, the war chief. Seattle wished to be brave, but when night came, he'd lay on the top platform and cover his head with the fur of a bear, terrified at the thought of war and torture.

In the spring of his seventh year, Seattle was glad winter was over. The people of his tribe were going camping. They'd move from place to place until the berries were gone in the fall. There was great activity around the village. Braves inspected nets, mats, fishing equipment, bows and arrows. Slaves scraped, painted, and polished canoes. Other slaves repaired tools and equipment. The squaws packed all possessions—everything but clothes. Indians wore all the clothes they owned.

On the first day, canoes were loaded with belongings, including women, children, and dogs. Chiefs Schweabe and Kitsap, medicine men, and subchiefs rode in the largest and best canoes. Slaves paddled the canoes. When, in perfect rhythm, the paddles cut the water, the Indians chanted eerie melodies as they went to their first campsite.

There, limbs were cut from trees to form the framework of temporary shelters for the night. Mats were thrown over the framework to provide protection from rain. When lice and fleas became unbearable, when disease appeared, or when the camp became excessively littered, the Indians moved on to a new location to continue gathering roots and berries.

# Chapter Two

## A Phantom Appears

Looking out over the water one day from a temporary island camp, the Indians of the Whulge saw a strange object appear on the horizon. As it grew larger and came closer, most of the Indians ran into the forest. Chiefs Schweabe and Kitsap and the warriors of the tribe remained on the beach, ready.

Instead of following his mother, Seattle edged over to his father's side. "Is it a phantom from the sky?"

"I think it's a big canoe, but stay close to my side," Schweabe said. "And do not be afraid."

"It doesn't have paddles," the boy said. "It has wings like a gull. I can see them move, and I can see spirits on the phantom. It might have flown to our waters."

All eyes were focused on the apparition as it came closer. Schweabe lifted his son to his shoulders to enable him to get a better view.

"It's turning," Seattle said. "A flying canoe coming this way, and it's folding its wings."

Silently the natives observed the wings.

"It's stopped," Kitsap said excitedly. "The phantom has stopped."

But it wasn't a phantom. It was the English man o' war *Discovery*, commanded by Captain George Vancouver. He was elated, for he believed he'd just made a historic discovery. He'd sailed into a great inland sea and named it Puget Sound.

The Indians standing on a beach of the Whulge had never seen a ship. They'd never seen a white man. Two Indians launched a canoe and begin paddling. The canoe circled the ship several times to scare away spirits. Then it came alongside the vessel. The Indians wouldn't venture aboard the ship, so the captain lowered gifts to show them he was a friend—gifts of

4

metal objects, beads, and blue cloth. The Indians accepted the gifts and made signs to show the captain they'd return.

Everyone became busy. Hunters went into the woods to kill deer. Some of the women and children picked berries, others dug large quantities of clams. The next day, braves carrying the food entered canoes to paddle toward the ship. The canoes circled the ship again and again while the braves chanted. Then they came alongside. Chief Kitsap, who knew many Indian dialects, boarded the boat.

Kitsap indicated that the canoes bore gifts of food. Hunters had killed a deer in the forest. There were clams from the sea and fresh berries from the land. Captain Vancouver accepted the gifts and invited all the Indians aboard. Schweabe then boarded the boat, leading a boy of seven by the hand. Vancouver recognized both Kitsap and Schweabe as the two chiefs who had circled the ship the day before. He greeted them, smiled at the little boy, and gave them gifts.

Other Indians boarded the vessel bearing food. They also received gifts and were allowed to wander over the ship. They were mystified at what they saw. Especially intriguing to them was the enormous amount of metal that had been used in the construction of the ship and in its guns and equipment. The Indians ate strange food and traded gifts, seeming to prefer ornamental objects to useful ones. The bartering continued as they entered their canoes for the return trip to the shore. Captain Vancouver smiled again at the little boy when he left the ship.

Kitsap was aboard the ship when it sailed away the next morning.

"Why did Kitsap go on the big canoe?" Seattle said.

"Kitsap talks many tongues. The big canoe wants to circle the Whulge while Kitsap scares away bad spirits," Schweabe said.

"Will he ever come back?"

"Yes, he'll come back when the bad spirits go away," the Suquamish chief said.

Chief Kitsap knew more dialects than any other man on the Whulge. Captain Vancouver recognized the Indian chief's linguistic ability. He wanted an interpreter, so he courteously invited the war chief to ride on the ship. Kitsap stayed with Vancouver while he explored and charted Puget Sound. When Chief Kitsap left the ship, the explorer presented him with metal tools.

In the years that followed, Seattle was often envious of Kitsap when he related events experienced on the great ship. Schweabe was envious to some extent also. He coveted the metal tools Captain Vancouver had given Kitsap, especially the knives Kitsap treasured and used the rest of his life.

Often the chief of the Suquamish tribe and his war chief talked about the white men who lived in lands far away.

"Why do Indians build little houses and paddle canoes while white men build hyas houses and hyas ships?" Schweabe said.

"We do not have metal," Kitsap said.

Schweabe glanced at the forests on the hills surrounding them. "We have the highest trees. Our enemies across the water have big canoes, big potlatch houses. Unlike the white man, those red men have only trees, no metal."

The enemy warriors lived on lands north of the Strait of Juan de Fuca. Among the coast Salish tribes, those who lived in British Columbia, had a more advanced civilization than the Indians who lived on Puget Sound. Their art was displayed with carvings and paintings on totem poles, feast dishes, and on ceremonial clothing and masks used in dances. These Indians built large decorated potlatch houses of cedar logs with roofs of hand-split cedar boards. The Haida and Tsimshian carved canoes from cedar logs. Their war canoes were often sixty or seventy feet long.

Some of the tribes that lived in British Columbia were rich, powerful warriors who secured slaves by swooping across the Strait of Juan de Fuca to battle tribes living on the shores of the Whulge.

The tribes of the Whulge feared those northern warriors. The two chiefs glanced apprehensively across the waters.

"You cannot build hyas potlatch house," Kitsap said.

Schweabe rose to his feet. He surveyed the foothills covered with enormous trees. He looked at the long, wide beach covered with clamshells, left by past generations of his people. He looked intently at the high bank above the beach. "The Suquamish tribe can build the biggest potlatch house of all."

"We can't fight our enemies with a hyas house. But with many hyas canoes; we could defeat any who should choose to attack us," said Kitsap.

"The ancestors of the Suquamish have dwelt on this beach since the sun first made light. We'll stay here as long as the sun shines in a house that we will build—a hyas house for all Suquamish. See that bank? See those trees?" Schweabe pointed to a bank nearby. "We can make big posts from the trees and set them in the sand in front of the bank."

Schweabe walked along the beach toward the water for about sixty feet. "This far from the bank."

He picked up a stick and drew an outline of a house in the sand. He indicated that when the posts were set in the sand, rafters made from big trees could be put from the bank to the top of the posts. Thus, they could form the framework of the house, which, he told Kitsap, could be covered with split planks. Mats could serve to partition the large building.

"The Suquamish can't do it. The Haida and Tsimshian have many slaves. Suquamish have few slaves."

Schweabe looked stunned. "You're wrong. I'm chief of the Suquamish, and we're going to build the greatest of all potlatch houses. We'll call it Tsu-Suc-Cub. You're war chief of the Suquamih tribe. Get the slaves."

Chief Schweabe selected a good site on which to build a potlatch house: a high bank on which grew enormous trees and there stretched a wide sandy beach. He became the first logger on Puget Sound. He spent many months in the woods where his slaves cut and burned enormous trees. They whacked off the limbs of trees. They cut bark off logs, scraping some logs and splitting others until they had enough logs and lumber to build an enormous structure.

# Chapter Three

# A Luminous Sea Gull

Chief Schweabe always feared an attack from the north. When Seattle was fourteen years old, his father said, "Some day, after the potlatch house is completed, you may be chief of all tribes on the Whulge. Many battles you will fight. Go into the woods, search for a powerful war spirit. Victory in war you must have, or warriors from the north will destroy the Suquamish potlatch house."

Seattle looked at the piles of timbers, thought of the work it had taken to prepare the logs, and thought of the work yet to be done. "I will be brave, father. I will search for a powerful spirit so I can defend our people as long as I live."

"I can't go into the woods to search for a powerful spirit because I fear not the creatures of the forest," Seattle thought. "My arrows shoot straight and they kill the hyas snarling creatures that roam high in the mountains. Cannibal women who dwell deep in the woods flee from me. I have never seen one. I have no fear of them."

He looked at a huge rock in the distance. It was a stormy day. The storm and tide threw giant waves against the rock.

"I must get ready to search for a spirit in the sea. I fear high tides that throw giant waves into the air. I fear horrible hyas slimy creatures that dwell deep in the sea."

The boy fasted for a long time, went through endurance tests, and rubbed his body with cedar bark so he'd be clean when he searched for a spirit that would guide his life. He dove into the ocean daily, stayed under water for long periods of time.

One day, early in the morning, he climbed a high cliff. He looked down at the sea that had become calm. He dove into the depths of the ocean. Down he sank. Horrible creatures of the deep surrounded him, but they passed by him. His spirit was not

9

there. He fought his way back to the surface and to the beach and dropped exhausted on the sand. He wished he could stay there forever, but after resting briefly, he stood up and wearily climbed toward the top of the cliff. He felt so faint he dropped down on the edge of a bank to rest while he watched the tide come in. He saw the waves rolling along the shore. Then he saw nothing because dizziness overcame him and he collapsed.

When the boy regained consciousness, he was lying on warm sand. The blue dome of the sky was over his head. A large, luminous sea gull circled over his head. Its wings flashed in the moonlight. He knew it was the spirit of the sea gull, the spirit of peace.

But the bewildered boy could not believe what his eyes saw. He closed them for an instant, but there was no mistake. There, standing on an upright timber, was an ethereal sea gull. The bird spoke to him, then vanished. All other birds disappeared too. Seattle was overjoyed. He had found the spirit of the sea gull, the spirit of peace. Never during his entire life did he tell what the spirit said. He didn't want to lose the power of peace.

Seattle seldom went north or west. He preferred to go across the Whulge to Duwamish territory to visit his cousins. As they grew older, Seattle and his Duwamish cousins liked to hunt in the dense forests covering the foothills east of the Whulge. Seattle developed his legs and his body by hiking over land and up mountains. When he reached manhood, he was a distinguished-looking, well-built, powerful man. He was six feet tall. With one blow of his fist he could knock down any member of his tribe. He had a quick temper, but he was not a fighter. He was a peaceful man.

Seattle's mother taught him to speak the Duwamish language fluently, a language he considered more beautiful than any other. Wherever he went, he was always treated with the courtesy due the son of the chief of the Suquamish tribe and the grandson of the chief of the Duwamish tribe. Whenever he stayed in a village, he always spoke to the people of the village and he always had an audience, even though many of the people who listened to him didn't understand the Duwamish dialect. They listened intently, hypnotized by the melody of his voice.

# Chapter Four

# Tsu-Suc-Cub

On one occasion, when Seattle returned from a hunting trip, his father met him as he beached his canoe.

"Come into the house," Schweabe said. "Kitsap and I want to talk with you."

Chief Kitsap was sitting on a platform when they entered the building.

"The pillars for Tsu-Suc-Cub are all in place, wedged in with stone and sand," Schweabe said. "All other timbers are ready, but the beams can never be lifted and put on top of the pillars. We've tried and tried, but our men are not strong. What can we do?"

"I have told you what to do," Kitsap said. "Stop building a big house and build war canoes out of those trees—big canoes. Then we can beat our enemies."

Seattle turned to Chief Kitsap. "When you were a boy, you found the spirit of bravery. That is well because victory in battle we must have, but use your war spirit when a war spirit is needed to protect the Suquamish tribe. I'll help the chief of our tribe build a hyas potlatch house."

"How can you help?" Kitsap said.

"I can help my father give a big potlatch."

"We can't give a big potlatch," Schweabe said. "We don't have gifts or food."

"Come outside, I will explain. We'll get the gifts and food, and the potlatch will lift the timbers because I have magical powers from the heavens. A powerful spirit became my guardian spirit when I was a boy. He spoke to me, and now that I am a man I know what the message he gave me means, listen!"

A melodious voice seemed to come from the heavens, calling all Indians to come at once. The mystified chiefs saw their tribesmen coming from every direction. The Indians watched the heavens for some further sign. Seattle raised his arms to command silence and spoke in the same melodious voice that had come from the sky.

"I speak for my father, chief of the Suquamish Indians, and for Chief Kitsap, our brave warrior. They want me to announce that they have just made me a subchief."

The Indians nodded to indicate approval. Seattle noticed the astonishment on the faces of Schweabe and Kitsap.

"Chief Schweabe wishes me to tell you that a magical spirit came to me from the heavens—the powerful spirit of the luminous sea gull," Seattle said.

The Indians had never heard of a luminous sea gull, but immediately they swayed back and forth, beating their heads against the ground. Seattle watched them for a few minutes, then continued.

"My father wishes me to tell you he will give the biggest of all potlatches to welcome the spirit of the luminous sea gull into our tribe."

Both fascination and consternation were written on the faces of Schweabe and Kitsap. The Indians seemed stupefied.

A medicine man jumped to his feet, pointing toward the sky. "The sea gulls."

A large flock of sea gulls were circling around and around overhead. Pandemonium broke loose. Shouting joyously, the Indians danced and sang. Chief Kitsap came forward to ask Seattle to stop the demonstration. "It's not possible to give a big potlatch."

Seattle looked straight at Kitsap. "Sit down on that log. It's the spirit of the sea gull that speaks, not I." Seattle turned again to watch the Indians dance and sing. Again he raised his arms. Again there was complete silence. "Our brave Chief Kitsap wishes to announce that he'll go forth to invite our friends to the potlatch. He'll first invite our Duwamish friends because my mother came to us from the Duwamish tribe." The Indians nodded as they glanced at Seattle's mother.

"He'll invite the Nisquallies."

All the Indians knew friendship existed between the Suquamish and Nisqually tribes, so again they showed their approval.

"He'll invite the Skykomish, Snohomish, Puyallup, Muckleshoot, Chehalis, and perhaps other tribes to the greatest of all potlatches. We'll have the biggest of everything. Biggest prizes, most gifts, biggest feasts. We'll have the greatest of all sports, the lifting of heavy weights. We'll give our largest and best canoe to the tribe that can lift our biggest beam and put it on top of our highest pile. We'll give big prizes to all tribes with strong men."

Seattle stood erect. "We'll know which tribe has the strongest men when all of those beams are on top of all those piles."

The cheering was deafening. Seattle again raised his arms to command silence. "To give biggest potlatch, we must have biggest gifts, most gifts, most food. You, our hunters, go into the forest to get skins and game. You, our fishermen, go to the ocean for big prizes—furs from the sea otter, oil from the whale. You, who fish in rivers and lakes, catch salmon and trout. Food, much food we must have." He paused for a moment. "You, the old men, fashion bows and arrows and spears. Women, weave mats and baskets. Everyone, dig clams, pick berries. Children, search beaches for unusual objects that come in with the tide. Many gifts we must have for biggest of all potlatches."

The Indians were still dancing and singing when Seattle left to go into the home of his father. Schweabe, the great Indian chief, was crying.

Seattle spoke softly. "You'll complete the building of Tsu-Suc-Cub. Suquamish tribe will have big house as long as you live, as long as I live."

14

It came to pass that the Indians on the Whulge lifted the beams to the top of the piles, a heroic feat.

Tsu-Suc-Cub was the largest Indian structure in the United States. It stretched along the beach for nine hundred feet. The seventy-four pillars along the front of the building were sunk deep in the sand. Their bases were from four to seven feet in diameter. They stood fifteen feet above the sand of the beach. Beams sixty-five feet long extended from the pillars to a bank ten feet high. The building, which covered an acre and a quarter of land, was covered with split planks three or four feet wide and three to five inches thick. Inside the potlatch house, two platforms, one above the other, stretched around the four walls. Spacious storage bins were installed above the platforms.

The house had forty compartments, each with its own stone fireplace. Smoke escaped through holes in the roof. Figures ornamented the seventy-four pillars along the front of the building. The corner ones were decorated with carved thunderbirds, brightly painted.

# Chapter Five

# Thunderbirds

The Indians believed the thunderbird had the power of thunder and lightning. Perhaps it did, for it was not long after the potlatch house was completed that the marauders from the north appeared in large war canoes. Each canoe carried from fifty to sixty painted warriors.

Kitsap saw the warriors approaching. Women and children, who ordinarily hid in the woods when strangers were sighted, ran into the potlatch house instead. Inside the building, braves stood ready with bows and arrows. The potlatch house became a fortress.

The invading warriors landed their canoes, started across the beach and saw the brilliantly painted thunderbirds. At the same instant arrows, like streaks of lightning, shot through the cracks in the huge building. The surprised warriors raised their bows.

"Shoot the thunderbirds!" shouted an enemy medicine man.

Arrows from Tsu-Suc-Cub whizzed through the air. It looked to the frightened attackers as if all the spirits pictured on the pillars were shooting at them. The warriors dropped their bows and spears and ran. They jumped into canoes and sped northward so fast that the spray caused by the paddles sent rainbows leaping into the air.

When the last canoe disappeared, men, women, and children rushed from the potlatch house shrieking and screaming. They picked up clubs and ran along the beach pounding piles of driftwood to scare away all evil spirits still lurking behind the timbers. To add to the confusion, the dogs also ran along the beach howling and barking.

Injured warriors left behind were carried into a compartment of Tsu-Suc-Cub where they were laid on mats on the floor. Those who survived became slaves.

16

The day ended with a feast. Then victorious braves danced their war dances and chanted war songs while the chiefs entered the house to sit around the campfires.

"They'll never attack us again," Chief Kitsap said.

"You are wrong," Seattle said. "Those northern Indians have the spirit of war. They have enormous canoes, so they will come back in warpaint to attack other tribes as well as our tribe. They will kill our women and children. Our warriors will become their slaves if the Indians of the Whulge do not prevent such cruel wars."

"How do you think war can be prevented?" Schweabe said. "The Duwamish, our friends across the Whulge, are mighty. They have many warriors, but they can't defeat the northern Indians."

"And all we could do today was to hide in Tsu-Suc-Cub," Kitsap said. "A big house won't stop those canoes forever. We must build big war canoes so that we have power to go after our enemies and defeat them."

Seattle smiled. "I have the power to stop those northern Indians, a magical power. I can always talk. Tomorrow morning at sunrise I will cross the waters to visit Duwamish Indians to tell them how the spirit of peace can defeat the spirit of war. My voice will be clear as I travel to visit other tribes. Many times the sun will light the mountains before I return, so I bid you good-bye for now."

The Indians of the Duwamish tribe recognized Seattle at once the next morning when he beached his canoe on their shore. He'd crossed the Whulge frequently to talk with their chiefs. Even as a little boy, he'd often visited them with his mother. The Indians were accustomed to seeing him, but his towering figure never failed to cause apprehension whenever he appeared on Duwamish soil. Su-quardle, the chief who welcomed him, liked to talk with Seattle because he spoke the Duwamish dialect. Seattle told Chief Su-quardle that Indians from the north had landed on the beach in front of Tsu-Suc-Cub. He described

17

how the invaders had fled, though it was evident they'd planned to attack the Suquamish tribe.

"The northern Indians were in warpaint, so I know they will attack us again," Seattle said. I am sure they'll attack other tribes as well, even a tribe as strong as the Duwamish. If they attack, you alone can't defeat them." Seattle then suggested that the tribes of the Whulge form an alliance to fight together and defeat the northern red men. "The Suquamish and Duwamish won't fight together cooperatively," Su-quardle said. "They would like to fight each other. Your plan is no good."

"No, chief, you are wrong. Our tribes will fight together because I intend to form a federation of tribes for the protection of all the Indians on our Whulge. I'm going from tribe to tribe to talk with the chiefs and their followers, and you know I have a loud voice."

The Duwamish chief laughed. "Never will the Duwamish join with Suquamish to beat in battle our common enemies, but I will call a powwow so you can talk. I warn you, however, if you are not careful, the Duwamish will be painting their faces black by the light of the moon and, before the sun rises, your Chief Kitsap will be on the warpath fighting us."

"The Duwamish and Suquamish are friends. Never again will they go to war against each other," Seattle said.

The subchiefs were not surprised to be called to hear the words of Seattle. They sat around him to listen.

Seattle's voice was low but emphatic. "I come to warn you. Our enemies from the north are on the warpath again. Yesterday morning, we saw their enormous war canoes off our shores. Our old men, our women and children hid in Tsu-Suc-Cub when we first sighted them. Our braves, under the leadership of Chief Kitsap, took positions at the front, inside the building. We were ready for them. We could see the warpaint on their faces when they beached their canoes.

"Slowly they started across the sands of the beach. Kitsap suddenly gave a signal. I sent my voice into the clouds so it

18

sounded like thunder. At the same instant our braves bombarded the invaders with arrows shot through the cracks of the potlatch house. An unseen enemy the northern warriors could not face, so they turned and fled in terror, but we know they'll come again to wage war on us because they have the spirit of war. Perhaps they will attack you the next time they swoop down in the darkness of night.

"The Suquamish, fighting alone, can't defeat them next time. Neither can the Duwamish, nor can any other tribe on the Whulge. What are you going to do? Are you going to watch your old men tortured, your women and children killed? Do you want to go north to become slaves?"

The Indians shook their heads vigorously. They all began to talk at once. Chief Seattle raised his arm. Everyone became silent.

"The Duwamish and Suquamish are big tribes, but even together we cannot beat our northern enemies, Seattle said. "If several tribes on the Whulge form an alliance, we'll have many canoes and many warriors. The Suquamish tribe has a chief with a powerful war spirit. Chief Kitsap could lead the Duwamish and Suquamish and allied tribes north to wage war on our common enemy, and we'd return to the Whulge victorious.

"My father and our war chief have just made me a subchief. We ask you to join us because I have a spirit that will help us defeat the spirit of war. I found it when I was a boy. You who have hunted with me know I fear not the cannibal women who dwell deep in the forest. I do not fear the cougar. I do not fear any spirit that stalks through the woods. I wondered where I would go to find a spirit invincible enough to defeat the spirit of war. The answer to that question was in front of me. It was a high cliff against which gigantic waves lashed the shore. I feared those rolling breakers. I feared the creatures of the deep, the lashing of the tails of whales battled by our fishermen. I knew from experience the strength in the arms of an octopus, but I climbed the cliff and jumped.

"A horrible creature started toward me, turned, and left. I knew then that my guardian spirit was not in the ocean. The force of the waves washed me ashore because I awoke at night lying on warm sand. I closed my eyes for a time. When I opened them, a giant bird flew across the face of the moon. It came to my side. It spoke to me. It was the spirit of the luminous sea gull. It's the spirit of peace that is speaking to you tonight."

Seattle raised his arm and pointed upward. The Indians looked at the sky and saw a mass of sea gulls flying northward.

Su-quardle jumped to his feet. "You've spoken for Kitsap, your war chief. I, too, have the spirit of war, so I say we will go north with Kitsap, your war chief. We'll kill women and children, burn homes. We'll steal the giant war canoes of the Haida and Tsimshian and bring them to the Whulge loaded with booty and slaves."

The Duwamish chief stopped talking because no one was listening to him. All eyes were watching a sign in the sky. Seattle's hand was raised, pointing to a billowy white cloud that had just drifted across the face of the moon. To the Indians, the cloud looked like a misty white apparition as it sailed above the sea gulls. Then it stopped, to drift downward until it enveloped the beautiful birds in a mantle of white. The Indians stood perfectly still, watching the cloud until it disappeared, moving steadily toward the north.


Months passed before Seattle beached his canoe in front of Tsu-Suc-Cub. He'd walked miles upon miles. He'd talked until he'd formed an alliance of six tribes called the Duwamish Confederation of Indians.

Seattle did not enter the potlatch house at once. Instead, he looked at the scenery surrounding his home. Looking westward, he could see a forest that his tribes didn't enter—a mysterious forest over which loomed a range of mountains covered with perpetual snow. Looking eastward across the water, he saw the sun rise over the mountains, which stretched as far as the eye could see.

Seattle and his hunters had penetrated these mountains. For generations his tribe had established beaver traps on the rivers in the valleys. They'd killed grizzlies and cougar for furs, bear, deer, and elk for food. The women of Seattle's tribe had camped along the rivers in the valleys to dig edible roots and to pick berries. They'd even gone as high as the mountain meadows to gather food.

For generations, Salish Indians had delighted in the beauty of the mountains. Seattle, viewing the mountains could see toward the north, Kulshan rising above other snow-clad peaks. Toward the south, he could see Tahoma, the highest mountain, called God by the Indians.

Seattle glanced toward the heavens and saw, in the brilliant sky, a lone luminous sea gull flying high above him. Upon perceiving it, he experienced a feeling of comfort and peace in the realization that he was home again after so long a time away.

"As long as I live, no enemy of my tribes will take Tsu-Suc-Cub or this spot of land from my people."

He entered the potlatch house to tell Chief Schweabe and Chief Kitsap that he had been successful, that the Duwamish, Suquamish and four other tribes had accepted the strategy of the plan. The Indians agreed not to wage war on each other and only to wage war on northern or eastern tribes when those tribes put on warpaint and attacked one of the tribes living on the Whulge.

# Chapter Six

# A Bold Adventure

Months passed without trouble. Then, one day, word came that northern Indians in warpaint had landed at Salmon Bay. Indians living nearby had been slaughtered. The plunderers journeyed north with many slaves. A short time after news of the massacre reached the Suquamish tribe, some canoes left its shores. At the same time, canoes left the shores of the Duwamish tribe.

The first canoes held Chiefs Kitsap, Seattle, Schweabe, and Su-quardle. Scores of other canoes filled with hundreds of warriors joined. Some canoes carried large quantities of arms, others carried abundant supplies of smoked and dried food.

The warriors of the Whulge, paddling their canoes toward the unknown territory, were frightened and tensed until Chief Seattle pointed out a flock of sea gulls flying northward high in the sky. Chief Seattle sang Duwamish melodies. Other Indians joined him, as the canoes passed villages along the shores.

Each night canoes were beached and their occupants slept on mats alongside them. On and on the caravan of canoes traveled among the many islands of the Whulge.

Late one day they entered a bay, on the shore of which they saw some buildings.[1]

---

[1] At about the time Captain Vancouver was charting Puget Sound, the Spaniard Lieutenant Salvador Fidalgo entered the Strait of Juan de Fuca and proceeded to the Bay of Munez Gaona, now called Neah Bay. There, in the early spring, he founded a military post with necessary buildings and fortifications. The post was established to fortify and help control the entrance to the strait. When fall came, however, winds and waves convinced the Spaniards that the site was ill adapted for a fort. They abandoned it, retreating to the trading post at Nootka across the strait on Vancouver Island, leaving the stockade to weather in the wind and rain.

"What can that be?" the braves said.

"It looks like a big potlatch house without a roof," Chief Schweabe said.

"It is the home of evil spirits. Evil spirits do not need a roof," a warrior said.

Kitsap and Seattle, like their tribesmen, were puzzled.

"What shall we do?" asked the war chief.

"I'll investigate," Seattle said. "I will land my canoe and track through the forest until I can see what is behind those timbers. Keep all canoes on the water until I send word how to proceed. Stay beyond the receding tide."

Seattle and two scouts beached a canoe out of sight. They went ashore, disappearing into the forest. Later, from the vantagepoint of the highest tree, they were able to view the sky, sea, and land all around. An Indian camp was inside the stockade. Apprehensively, the Indians inside were watching the armada of canoes tossing on the waves. From the treetop, Seattle and the scouts could see women and children piling driftwood and trash against a large gate that opened inward, thus preventing entrance. Anxious braves were inspecting their weapons of warfare.

"Far too many warriors for a village so small," Seattle thought. Looking toward the west, he saw the Pacific Ocean for the first time in his life. The Big Water seemed even more expansive than he'd imagined.

He also saw a sight that startled him. Huge war canoes were nestled in a sheltered cove some distance away. "Those canoes belong to our enemies from the north. The warriors in that village are the ones who waged war at Salmon Bay. Now they are preparing their own trap, for just as no one can enter the stockade, also no one can exit. We will get them. We will conquer all of them. Then we'll capture the huge war canoes."

Seattle directed the scouts to watch the happenings inside the stockade while he went to inform the war chief.

Seattle paddled across the water and climbed into Kitsap's canoe. The two chiefs conferred for a long time. At last the canoes began to move.

Warriors of the Confederation seized their sleeping mats, ran past the campfires to light the mats, and tossed them blazing over the walls of the stockade. The heaps of dry driftwood piled against the gate and the houses in the village quickly caught fire. The scouts climbed down the tree to join their tribesmen on the beach. As they wound their way through the forest, they heard the screams of the trapped victims. Very few were strong and agile enough to climb the timbers of the stockade to escape into the woods.

Flames were leaping high above the stockade, billows of smoke spreading out over the ocean.

Seattle joined the scouts. "Did you see the war canoes in the cove above here?"

The two scouts nodded.

"Do you think you can find them?"

"We can find them. Big war canoes of our enemies."

"Our war chiefs are going after those canoes with many warriors." Seattle pointed along the shore to Chiefs Kitsap and Su-quardle, who were surrounded by about two hundred warriors. "Go with our war chiefs to guide them to the cove. I'll remain with the rest of our people. Chief Kitsap will be joyous, for now he'll have huge war canoes."

Seattle saw the warriors enter their canoes and start west. Then he walked quietly up the shore to join his tribesmen, who were standing in groups along the beach. Some of them were looking at the warriors in the canoes, others were watching the flames eating into the abandoned stockade. Many seemed stunned. Others were talking. Seattle knew all were frightened. He knew they wished to return to the Whulge.

He raised his arms and stood still until the Indians gathered around him. He spoke to them in a quiet, consoling voice. "My people from the Whulge, you have just witnessed the horrible cruelty of war. Many men, women, and children died in the fire. Only a very few of the strongest men scaled that barrier and fled into the woods. War I loathe, but we must go on when the sun rises again, on and on to a setting sun where live other of our enemies. There we must capture or destroy their war canoes so that never again can they put on war paint and heap the horrors of war on our people.

"You know I went ashore a while ago. I climbed a giant tree, and from its top I saw behind the wooden barrier. I saw enemy warriors who had just returned from our Whulge, the enemies who killed our people at Salmon Bay. From that treetop I saw, hidden in a cove, war canoes that can hold many warriors. Chief Kitsap has gone after those canoes. He will return at sunrise. Then we'll get ready to paddle the captured canoes toward a setting sun to vanquish in battle all our ancient enemies."

The chief sat down on a log while his tribesmen wandered up and down the beach talking to each other.

Chief Seattle jumped to his feet. "Fish, a big school of them. See them jump!"

Followed by his tribesmen, Chief Seattle ran to the water's edge where they all talked excitedly as they watched the unusual disturbance on the sea.

"Catch them," the chief said. "Many fish, many are big fish. Catch them for a hiya muckamuck."

Fishermen of the tribe jumped into canoes as fast as they could launch them. Indians left on the shore anxiously watched the canoes of the fishermen.

"We must build ovens, large ovens for big fish. Come with me," Seattle said.

The chief, followed by tribesmen, walked toward the bank. "Dig here. Above the line of the high tide, all along the beach."

The Indians dug deep pits in the sand, lining the pits with rocks. They gathered driftwood and built fires on top of the rocks. Then, when the fires were blazing, the Indians went to the water's edge to watch the activity on the water, until, at dusk, the fishermen came ashore with a huge catch of fish.

Ashes were brushed from the hot rocks. Fish were laid in the hot ovens. Seaweed was put on top of the fish. The pits were filled with small rocks, and new fires were built on top of the buried fish.

The Indians stretched out on the warm sand to sleep. They knew the fish in the rock ovens would bake during the night.

Seattle scanned the ocean, looked along the beaches, observed the dying embers of the burned fort, and then beyond the fort at the forest. "Many people perished horribly. Some few managed to escape into the woods. Long ago when I was still a boy, a sea gull, my guardian spirit, told me that in my manhood years I'd be a power for peace. That there be peace as long as there is time on Suquamish and Duwamish lands is my fervent hope."

He stood and looked up at the sky. A sympathetic, soothing voice came from above. The exhausted braves lying on the beach heard, "Night is here, sleep in peace."

Seattle walked behind a pile of driftwood, drew a blanket close around his body, and slept soundly until he heard shouting.

"Kitsap is coming. Su-quardle is coming. They have gigantic war canoes," someone said.

Seattle came from his hiding place. His tribesmen, shouting, were running along the beach. Some of them had reached the area where canoes could be pulled ashore. Chief Seattle greeted the war chiefs while excited Indians pulled the canoes on the beach. Many of the Indians had never seen such large canoes.

"We give to you, our victorious warriors, a great welcome and hiya muckamuck. See the ovens along the shore," Seattle said.

Shouting Indians rushed to the ovens and removed the rock and seaweed to uncover the steaming fish. The famished men devoured large hunks of fish. They ate until they could eat no more.

"We have captured many war canoes, but complete victory we must have. The sun is high in the sky, so we must go on now to the homes of our enemies to destroy them," Kitsap said.

Intent upon eating, the Indians had paid no attention to the sky. Now they peered upward through the hazy atmosphere. The heavens, clear to the horizon, were covered with a mystical brilliance the Indians had never before seen. The howl of a wolf was heard. It seemed to come from the crimson clouds. The warriors rushed to the water's edge, rapidly loaded the canoes, and jumped into them. Then, led by the war chiefs, they paddled north. On and on they went until they reached the shores of their enemies.

The northern tribes didn't expect an invasion by warriors from the south and weren't prepared for war. Never had Indians from the Whulge come to their shores. Complete disorder developed as they watched the approach of the massive flotilla of canoes filled with painted warriors. To add to the feeling of panic, the northern Indians recognized their own canoes among those of the Whulge. Braves, women, and children left all possessions and fled into the forest. Those who had journeyed so far to vanquish their enemies found no one to kill. The village was completely abandoned, save for barking dogs.

A war council was held. They'd come to massacre and they found no one to kill. But plunder they could. Braves searched for possessions. Rapidly they packed the loot in canoes.

Chief Schweabe was reluctant to wreck the houses, houses so much sturdier than any on the Whulge. Chief Seattle, however, insisted.

"We must burn all buildings," Seattle said. "We must take all canoes, everything of value. Complete victory we must have."

All about were elaborately carved totem poles. Chief Kitsap objected to destroying them.

"We can heap brush around totem poles and burn them," a subchief said.

"We can't burn totem poles with faces of ancestors of our enemies staring at us. Our braves would look at those faces, jump into the water and try to swim across the Big Water," Kitsap said.

Chief Seattle suggested that they let the poles stand. He realized the people who carved them were craftsmen of great ability. "Those carvers were not thinking of war when they carved those faces. They were thinking of the traditions of their people."

A distance away some enormous structures were seen. In front of each building was a huge totem pole, far larger and more elaborate than any they'd yet seen.

"That area is the burial place of this village," Seattle said.

The Indians became frightened.

Suddenly a clear voice seemed to come from behind the totem poles. "Paddle toward the setting sun."

Chief Kitsap, recognizing the mysterious voice to be that of Chief Seattle, shouted, "Run fast to the canoes."

The caravan of canoes began the journey amid songs of victory. They had far to go to reach their home shores, but the warriors were happy. They'd defeated their ancient enemies. They'd captured enormous war canoes. They were returning home with many other valuable spoils of war, furs of the otter, skins of other animals, bladders filled with whale oil, and prized hiaqua shells.

"We left our marauding enemies powerless," Seattle thought. "In fear, they ran from us, hid in the forest. No longer can they swoop down upon us in surprise attack to plunder and kill. Now we can live in peace."

# Chapter Seven

## Duwamish Princess

When Chief Schweabe appointed his son chief of the Suquamish tribe, the apartments in Tsu-Suc-Cub were reorganized. Chief Seattle was given the largest apartment, the one that had been his father's. Chief Kitsap, the war chief, retained the next largest. Chief Schweabe took a third apartment. These three sections of the potlatch house were armed. The remaining sections of the huge structure were allotted to subchiefs, medicine men, other warriors and their slaves according to their individual tribal status.

One day, Seattle's slaves loaded a canoe with rich furs and other spoils of war. Then they crossed the Whulge to Duwamish land. Seattle went at once to the home of a Duwamish chief.

"I bring rich gifts to you, a chief of your tribe," Seattle said. "I want to marry your beautiful daughter."

"Where are these gifts?" the astonished chief said.

"In my canoe off shore. You can inspect the beautiful furs and hiaqua shells. My slaves will bring them to you."

"Have you ever seen my lovely one?"

"For many years I've known your daughter. I knew her when we were children, when I visited Duwamish relatives with my mother. Then I met her again at the home of one of my cousins when I was a young man and she was a beautiful maiden. I walked home with her and I did not forget her."

Chief Seattle smiled. "Since then I have crossed the Whulge frequently to see your daughter. She has a lovely voice and I, too, have learned to sing your Duwamish melodies. Your young people travel upstream and downstream and sing with the beat of paddles. Your daughter always helped me paddle my canoe as we sang together, and she has known for a long time that

29

someday I would bring rich gifts to your door. Now I am chief of the Suquamish tribe, and I want your daughter for my wife."

The Duwamish chief was pleased. He had not realized his daughter knew the famous leader.

He was silent for a minute. "I will look at your gifts. They must be rich gifts because there is no fairer maid in all our lands."

"The gifts are rich and many, and when you see them, remember the Suquamish tribe has Kitsap, a powerful war chief. It will be well for the Duwamish and Suquamish tribes to remain friends."

The gifts were accepted. Two weeks later the chief of the Duwamish tribe crossed the water to present Seattle with gifts. During the weeks that followed there were frequent visits between members of the two tribes. Eventually, the Duwamish chief gave a big potlatch to which he invited chiefs of friendly tribes.

Chiefs bearing gifts came from far and near to attend the festivities of the marriage of a princess to the famous chief. There were sports, gambling, singing, and dancing. Then everyone gorged themselves on the plentiful feast given by the Duwamish chief.

When the day ended, Chief Seattle and his wife stepped into an elaborately carved canoe. Slaves paddled the canoe across the water to Tsu-Suc-Cub.

Seattle continued to hunt in the mountains. He visited other tribes, often accompanied by his young wife. Much of the time, however, he stayed at home with his own people, living prosperously and peacefully. His happiness was complete when a child was born. Her mother named the newly born princess Kick-is-om-lo.

One day, when Kick-is-om-lo was but a little girl, great sadness fell upon Seattle and his tribe. His young wife fell sick and died.  Happiness for Seattle was gone.  Leaving his little princess with his mother, Seattle left his home.  He traveled from tribe to tribe, leading the wild life of a gambler.  At times he went high in the mountains east of the Whulge where his slaves inspected the beaver traps while he and his subchiefs hunted for bear, deer, and cougar.  Indians everywhere respected Seattle, but they also feared him.  With brute strength he dealt out justice.  One blow with his fist sent a wrongdoer cowering to the ground.

Seattle returned to Tsu-Suc-Cub often to take Kick-is-om-lo with him into the woods to teach her the signs of the forest and how to handle a canoe when crossing the Whulge.  She learned to paddle the canoe and to shoot with bow and arrow as expertly as a boy.  She liked to cross the Whulge to visit relatives, for both her mother and grandmother had been Duwamish.  Seattle took her with him frequently so that she could play on the beach with her Duwamish cousins.

# Chapter Eight

# Cunning Strategy

One day Kick-is-om-lo saw her father hurry toward his canoe, so she followed him.

"No girls today," he said. "I go across the water for a big powwow."

The chief of the Suquamish tribe had been summoned to Duwamish territory because word had been received that mountain Indians were planning to attack the Indians on the Whulge. Su-quardle had called a powwow of chiefs and subchiefs of several tribes to discuss various methods of dealing with the hostile tribes.

Schweabe and Kitsap were away from home when the message arrived, but Seattle crossed the water at once and went directly to the home of the Duwamish chief. When he entered the building, he was greeted by Su-quardle and escorted to the place reserved for him, the leader of the tribes of the Whulge. A number of chiefs were in the council room awaiting his arrival. A roaring fire provided warmth and light. Smoke slowly filtered upward through openings in the roof.

Many plans for defeating the enemy were suggested by the assembled chiefs, but all seemed futile to Seattle because so many innocent, helpless people would suffer and die. Suddenly, Seattle sprang to his feet to speak. A hush settled over the council members as they listened to Seattle discuss the inevitable horror of a war on the Whulge.

"Even if we are victorious in the battle, many of the injured will be tortured, many will die. We must save our people. We must stop the mountain warriors before they reach our shores."

Seattle hesitated. "My friends of our allied tribes, we can stop them at the place where our lands meet their lands, at the junction where the streams from the mountains flow into the

Duwamish River. As I returned from my last hunting trip, I noticed big trees and dense underbrush at the point of convergence of the three rivers. The war canoes of our enemies must pass that spot, and there we must stop them."

A subchief rose to his feet. "Those mountain warriors may not pass the place where the rivers meet. They may sneak through the forest and surprise us in our villages. What will happen to those left behind if our warriors are far away at the headwaters of the Duwamish?"

"Mountain Indians have big canoes," Seattle said. They won't break their way through dense underbrush and woods when they can step into their canoes and be carried to our shores on the down current of a mountain stream."

Seattle looked at the subchief. "It will be well for many of our warriors to stay on the shores of the Whulge to protect our people, should our enemies from the north suddenly attack us. Prepare to defend yourselves against any possible attack. You can then battle any tribe that trespasses on Duwamish or Suquamish territory or on the territory of our allied tribes."

His listeners nodded. The door opened and Kitsap entered. Chief Seattle greeted the war chief of his tribe. Silence prevailed while the two chiefs conferred in the Suquamish dialect. Kitsap then left the room.

Again Seattle addressed the assembled chiefs. "Chief Kitsap thinks we can carry out a secret mission that will stop the mountain warriors on their own territory, preventing them from even reaching Duwamish lands."

Seattle turned to speak directly to two subchiefs, "You were with me on my last hunting trip. Do you remember the difficulty we had when we tried to go through the dense underbrush along the bank of the White River?"

"I remember the thorns that gouged us," one said.

"I remember the big tree that marked the place where we hid the canoe," the other said. Many trees there. No one could find a canoe there."

"Will you volunteer to go into the woods with me to meet the hostile foes?" Seattle said.

"We will go," the subchiefs said.

"Leave this council," Seattle said. "Get four hunters. Get a canoe ready for a hunting trip. I will meet you at the river."

The two chiefs left.

Seattle spoke to the remaining chiefs. "Warriors from Suquamish lands are crossing the Whulge at this moment to join Chief Kitsap. He'll need more men, warriors who are skilled woodsmen." Seattle pointed to two subchiefs, well-known scouts. "Go to Kitsap. Help him find among the Duwamish, warriors who know the woods."

Seattle turned to the Duwamish chief. "Guard your shores. Keep all plans secret. Pay no attention to hunters. Pay no attention to fishermen on the Duwamish River. Kitsap will be with them. But be ready to fight."

"We understand. We'll fight any enemy that approaches our beaches," Su-quardle said.

Seattle left the room.


It was almost dark when men, loitering on the riverbank, noticed some hunters get into a canoe.

"That's Chief Seattle," one man said. "He must be going on a hunting trip again. Great hunter he is, fears nothing. Last time he was in the mountains he shot a cougar that was killing a deer."

The canoe had scarcely disappeared when the men noticed fishermen on the river, but they paid no attention. Fishermen were a customary sight. The observers did not know that the Suquamish war chief was one of those fishermen.

The men were more interested in two canoes that were turning and twisting while their occupants apparently were having fun. They seemed to be trying to best each other as they skillfully battled both a down current on the Duwamish River and an incoming tide from the ocean. The idlers did not know that the bottoms of those two canoes carried tools of woodsmen and implements of war.

The hunters and fishermen paddled quietly as they went upstream, attentive to unusual sounds. They heard nothing but the infinite silence of a vast wilderness broken only by the noise of rushing streams of water and by wind whistling in the treetops.

Seattle and his companions were the first to reach the fork in the river, the spot where the mountain streams met to form the headwaters of the Duwamish River. However Kitsap and the warriors arrived soon after the hunters beached their canoe.

The men climbed the bank of the river. It wasn't long until Kitsap, the warriors and canoes disappeared into the woods.

"This is the tree. Can you do it?" Seattle said.

"It's perfect. The tree leans slightly toward the river. The wind is with us."

The woodsmen began working on the tree. With tools made of bone, they hacked and scraped until they'd scaled the bark from the base of the side of the tree that faced the river. A woodsman built a small fire against the bared trunk. Using watertight baskets, other woodsmen dipped water from the river and placed it near the tree so that the fire could be controlled. For hours, the men hacked at the tree, burning its side, and scraping the charred wood.

In the east, the sky turned to shades of red and gold as a rising sun cast a glow over the snow-covered mountains. At last the tree was prepared. A huge gaping cavity split the side that faced the river. Several strong Indians came from the woods to take the place of those who'd labored until dawn. The most expert woodsman of the Suquamish tribe, a man who'd helped build Tsu-Suc-Cub, directed them. Wedges made of bone were inserted in the immense breech. The bone wedges were pounded with rock sledges. For hours the Indians hacked and pounded.

In the late afternoon, Seattle came from the forest to inspect the progress.

"It will not be long now," the head woodsman said. "Kitsap, better get men back out of the way."

Whang! Whang! Whang! resounded through the forest. Crack—Cr-a-ck!

"Run!" shrieked the woodsman. Everyone fled to a place of safety. Limbs of nearby trees spun into the air as a giant of the forest crashed, falling directly across the river.

The warriors gathered to marvel at the achievement. The tree and a mass' of underbrush blocked the river at the point where the lands of the mountain Indians joined the lands of the Duwamish. Nothing could pass that barricade save running water.

Seattle spoke quietly, but clearly. "Hide and wait."

The men faded into the surrounding woods. Silence reigned.

It was almost dusk when the warriors heard the faint sound of paddles cutting the water. Two canoes of warriors came into view, closely followed by other canoes. Rounding the bend in the river, the invaders saw the barricade too late. Their canoes hit the submerged tree and capsized, sending the occupants sprawling into a tangled mass of broken tree limbs and underbrush covered with thorns. Kitsap howled like a wolf, the battle cry of the Suquamish.

Many of the enemy drowned. Those who were able to swim to the shore were killed or captured. Two canoeloads of warriors saw the trap in time to avoid it. Deftly turning their canoes, they escaped upstream.

To portage the captured canoes, Kitsap had a path cleared on the bank at the end of the fallen tree. Then the canoes of the mountain Indians were lowered into the waters of the Duwamish River, and the assemblage of canoes glided swiftly down the stream.

Chiefs and warriors guarding the shores of the Whulge saw Chiefs Seattle and Kitsap riding at the head of the captured war canoes. The howl of the wolf rent the air, followed by the cry of victory.

Seattle's strategy had stopped a destructive war on the shores of the Whulge. He was made chief of the Duwamish tribe, and Su-quardle became a subchief. A short while later Seattle was awarded a distinction he had dreamed of attaining even as a little boy. Because his strategies had defeated both the enemies from the north and the enemies from the east, he was elected chief of an alliance of the six tribes that had outmaneuvered the mountain Indians, an alliance known as The Duwamish Federation of Six Tribes. Never again in his entire life did Seattle actively engage in warfare. Although he had a quick temper and was powerful physically, he was dominated by the spirit of the sea gull. As the years passed he remained the most powerful chief on the Whulge and a great advocate of peace.

# Chapter Nine

## Kick-is-om-lo

Tsu-Suc-Cub was Seattle's home. He married a second time, a Suquamish maid, and by her had two sons known to the white man as George and Jim. Kick-is-om-lo, his reckless, untamed daughter, was more of a companion to him than his sons. She accompanied him on many of his journeys. Proud of her father, she never failed to express her admiration for him.

One day Dokum Cud, a noted warrior, approached the Suquamish shore on a peaceful mission.

"Tell Chief Dokum Cud I am honored, Seattle said to the messenger. "I welcome the friendly visit of the great chief of the Skagits."

Dokum Cud accepted the invitation to enter the potlatch house. Slaves carrying rich gifts followed him, gifts of sea-otter skins, blankets made from the wool of mountain goats, and hiaqua shells.

The two chiefs didn't speak the same dialect, so an interpreter spoke to Seattle. "Chief Dokum Cud, of the Skagits, presents you with the rich gifts of his tribe. He wishes to marry your daughter."

Seattle was stunned for a minute. He had not thought about his daughter marrying anyone. "She is only a little girl," he thought. "I cannot arrange a marriage for her with the chief of a northern tribe."

The Skagit chief noticed Seattle's hesitation. Angered, he turned to speak to the interpreter.

"Chief Dokum Cud says his domain is large," the interpreter said. "It extends far to the north. He has a big potlatch house, many totem poles. His hunters kill game in the mountains. He has many rich furs. He's seen your daughter. He wishes to marry her. He will come again with more gifts. He will bring many hiaqua shells, richer furs, more blankets."

"Rich furs, soft blankets, many shells I will accept, but we must have a bigger bargain than riches," Seattle said.

The interpreter repeated what Seattle said. Dokum Cud listened, then said something. "What did Cud say?" Seattle said.

"He wants to know what is bigger than riches," the interpreter replied.

"Tell Cud he is a great warrior. He has waged war against some of my tribes and he has defeated them in battle. Tell him friendship is bigger than riches."

"The great chief of the Duwamish Confederacy is my friend now," Cud said. "I will marry his daughter."

Chief Seattle called a subchief and spoke to him. He then turned to the interpreter. "I have ordered food so that I can bargain with a friend until the sun rises."

When the Skagit chief left at daybreak he carried gifts from Seattle and he had agreed never to wage war on any tribe of the Duwamish Confederacy.

Seattle did not tell anyone he had promised his daughter to the chief of the Skagits. He didn't like to think of giving away his little girl in marriage. He loved her, but he knew she was old enough to marry and she, his daughter, must marry a great chief. Dokum Cud was a great chief, a rich one. The lands he ruled extended far to the north, encompassing a vast area.

It wasn't until Cud came again with richer gifts that Seattle called his daughter into the potlatch house to show her the gifts he'd accepted, to tell her that he had arranged her marriage to Dokum Cud.

"Cud is here now," Seattle said. "He wishes you to go with him when he returns north. I will give a potlatch and announce your marriage to the chief of the Skagits. You will live in big potlatch house and you'll be great lady like your grandmother and like your mother."

Kick-is-om-lo could hardly grasp what her father was telling her. She did not want to go and live with people she had always regarded as enemies. She wanted to live with her own people, either the Suquamish or the Duwamish. She looked at her father for a minute. "I will not marry the Skagit chief. I will not leave my own people."

"The chief of the Skagits is a brave warrior, a ruler of his people. My daughter must marry a great chief. The chief of the Skagits is great. I am your father and I have given you to him in marriage."

"Never will I marry the Skagits' chief."

Seattle's eyes flashed. "You will marry him. Get ready to go with him now. I'm going to announce your marriage to him at once."

Kick-is-om-lo had her father's temper. She walked over to the pile of gifts. She scattered them in every direction defiantly, then burst into tears and ran out of the potlatch house.

Seattle was upset. "I wish she was a boy. If she were a boy she could go high into the mountain peaks and find the spirit of the thunderbird. If she were a man, I could make her our war chief. But she is a woman and women cry."


The potlatch was held, the marriage knot tied, and Dokum Cud returned north to his home with his new bride. Seattle bade her goodbye with her promise that she would visit Tsu-Suc-Cub often.

Seattle became more and more uneasy when weeks and months passed by and Kick-is-om-lo didn't return to Tsu-Suc-Cub.

Then, one day, Seattle saw Dokum Cud. "I have taken my wife far to the north. She lives in a big potlatch house that is guarded by spirits whose pictures are carved on many totem poles."

Seattle was stunned. "You took her to the far north toward the land of darkness, away from all her people?"

"She is my wife," Dokum Cud said.

Even though he was greatly shocked, Seattle showed no emotion. He looked intently at Cud, bowed low to the chief, and walked away. Chief Seattle knew that never again would he see his little girl.


Many years later a weeping woman ran into Tsu-Suc-Cub and threw herself into the chief's arms. He did not recognize the haggard, exhausted woman until she spoke. "I have come back, papa. I paddled and paddled and now I'm here."

"You have come back from the far-away domain of the Skagits chief and you come alone," Seattle said. "How did you find your way?"

"The sun in the sky was my guide at first." Kick-is-om-lo pointed south, then west. "Then I saw Kulshan and I knew I was on the water of the Whulge. Then by the light of the big moon I saw Tahoma. I rejoiced for I knew I was near home."

"Many times I tried to come back, but always I was caught and taken back to Cud. He tortured me without mercy."

When Kick-is-om-lo described the brutal treatment she had received from her ruthless husband, Seattle's dark face turned white and his muscles became rigid. "Where is Cud?" he asked.

"My husband is dead. He was killed in a drunken brawl."

Chief Seattle put his arms around his daughter. "Never will I forgive myself for what I have done to you."

"But I am here at last, safe with you in Tsu-Suc-Cub."

Kick-is-om-lo looked around the room in the huge structure, then tears welled up and she became hysterical. Seattle held her in his arms. When she was quiet, he carried her across the room and put her gently on a pile of furs.

"Sleep here, my child," he said.

The exhausted woman fell asleep at once.

*Florence Westover Bond*

When she opened her eyes again, he spoke. "You have slept well while I've been thinking of days gone by. It does not seem possible that mistakes of the past disappear. Remember only that you are my daughter and you live in Tsu-Suc-Cub, the home of your people. You are again the princess of the Suquamish Indians."

# Chapter Ten

## Pale Face Comes to the Whulge

The Indians of the Whulge were isolated. However, as time passed, Seattle learned that warlike Indian tribes lived beyond both the Cascade and Rocky Mountains. Occasionally, the Klickitats came through the mountains and told tales of other tribes that made war on each other, tales of waterless deserts beyond. They told of prairies far away where Indians hunted buffalo and antelope. The stories were bewildering to the canoe Indians of the Whulge.

News filtered up to Seattle of the coming of white men to the big river. The knowledge he had was scant. Often, much information that came to him was little more accurate than vague rumor. He yearned for more accurate knowledge. He had heard of ships that sailed up the Columbia River. He knew a great company, the Hudson's Bay Company, had established a fur-trading post and fort a distance upstream on the big river. He knew the fort was called Fort Vancouver in honor of the captain who had sailed on the Whulge, when Seattle was a boy.

A white man who passed by Tsu-Suc-Cub one day described the fort to Chief Seattle. "There's many buildings in the fort. It's surrounded by a wall of upright logs called a stockade. Inside there's a large house for white-headed Eagle, the chief agent, and there's houses for others. There's all sorts of buildings inside, a large store house, a kitchen, a carpentry shop. Outside there's more shops, sheds, and houses. They've a store where red men bring furs to trade for blankets, tobacco, guns, and such things."

"Where does white-headed Eagle get all the supplies?" Seattle said.

"Some are brought from all across the country. Many supplies are raised on the land around the fort. But many more

43

are brought up the river by ship. White-headed Eagle is in charge of everything and everyone. He's fair in his dealings with red men and with white men."

The man told tales of life at the fort. Seattle found it hard to comprehend the stories. He longed to take a trip to Fort Vancouver to see for himself what the white man was so rapidly accomplishing. He was intrigued and mystified by the stories of the life and work of the white people who lived at the fort.

Often Seattle would scan the horizon. "Ships sail up the big river. Someday ships will come to the Whulge."

One day, when he was looking out over the water, Seattle saw two boys beach a canoe and come ashore. He walked along the beach to speak with the boys, who were about seventeen years of age. One of the boys could speak the Duwamish dialect.

"Pale faces come to Whulge. They built a house on the beach. A house this big." The boy walked about ten feet in one direction and about twelve feet in another.

"I have looked, but no canoes of white men have I seen," Seattle said.

"Not on water. Men walked from the big river. The big canoe of the white men come." The boy pointed north, gestured, then pointed toward the sun.

"How do you know the white man's canoe will come soon by water?" Seattle said. "Big canoe come, with goods to trade for furs?"

The boy indicated that a ship would come by water soon. "White man's goods." The boy again pointed north and again indicated that the white men who'd erected the house expected goods by boat, goods to trade for furs.

"Come into my house to rest while I give you food," Seattle said. The boys, who'd paddled their canoe a long distance, were very hungry. They devoured salmon and smoked deer meat. They ate a pastry-like bread and some dried berries.

The chief plied them with questions while they ate. "We paddled fast to tell the big chief of the Duwamish. I am Leschi, son of the chief of the Nisqually tribe. My father is hunting in the mountains, so we decided to come to Tsu-Suc-Cub."

Seattle learned that the boys were on a camping trip when they discovered the new log house built on an elevated part of the beach. The white men, seeing the boys, walked along the beach to talk with them. They showed the boys the house they'd built.

"You do well to tell me," Seattle said. "Go now to the platform to rest." He pointed to the upper platform where some furs were piled.

The boys were so tired they fell asleep at once and didn't awaken until dawn.

The chief was waiting for the boys when they started toward their canoe in the early morning. He gave them some strings of smoked clams to eat. "I'm going back with you. Come, the canoes are ready."

The boys walked rapidly, eating the clams, and started to get into their canoe. Seattle stopped them.

"You ride in my canoe," Seattle said. You direct me to the new house of the white man. Slaves will paddle your canoe back to Nisqually land."

While the boys slept, Seattle's slaves had equipped canoes for a camping trip. The canoes carried mats, furs, a bladder filled with fresh water, food, and fishing and hunting equipment.

Chief Seattle, one of his subchiefs, and the boys rode in the first canoe. The second canoe held camping equipment. The third, Indian braves. The boys' canoe, paddled by two slaves, came last. The boys were excited over going back to Nisqually land in the big canoe of the greatest chief on the Whulge. Upon reaching Nisqually territory, Chief Seattle observed that some Indians were preparing to camp on the beach some distance from the house built by the traders. Seattle ordered his slaves to pitch a camp on land close to the house on the beach.

The traders learned from Leschi that the greatest chief on the Whulge brought greetings to them, that his tribes would exchange furs for the white man's goods.

Seattle came from his tent. He was presented with gifts, and he, in turn, presented the traders with furs of the beaver. The traders rejoiced. The gift from Seattle was a good omen. The ship, expected to arrive within a day or two, was the *Beaver*, the first steamship on the Pacific Coast.

Upon its arrival, the captain invited Chief Seattle to come aboard to inspect the ship. Seattle was intrigued to learn from the captain that the large wheel turning round and round was a large paddle run by steam. The chief was overjoyed when, later, the captain invited him to ride back to Tsu-Suc-Cub on the ship.

Seattle did not realize that the arrival of the *Beaver* on the Whulge not only would change his life completely, but also would change the life of the boy, Leschi. He learned that white men called the Whulge "Puget Sound." He knew the white fur traders called Tsu-Suc-Cub "Old-Man-House," which, in Chinook jargon, meant big strong house.

The new log house on the Nisqually beach became the temporary quarters for the fur-trading business until the Hudson's Bay Company built Fort Nisqually, which like Fort Vancouver, had a stockade, two bastions and a heavy gate. A large store was erected inside the stockade where furs could be traded for white man's goods. Later, the fur traders built other structures, including a home for the chief agent, a granary, a blacksmith shop, and a cookhouse where bread was baked in a large dutch oven. The fort controlled one hundred sixty thousand acres of land along the shores of Puget Sound, land between the Nisqually and Puyallup Rivers, land so rich it was either cultivated or used for grazing. The Puget Sound Agricultural Company was formed to handle the raising of crops and domestic animals.

The *Beaver* became a busy steamer. For years, Seattle watched it pass Old-Man-House as it went to and from Fort

Nisqually. It carried grain and dairy products to British Columbia and to Alaska. It returned to Fort Vancouver loaded with furs, which were then shipped to foreign lands. The *Beaver* was a useful steamboat all during Chief Seattle's life.

# Chapter Eleven

## The Man in the Black Robe

Dr. William Tolmie was the chief agent and manager of affairs at Fort Nisqually. The settlers on lands neighboring the lower end of Puget Sound always could procure food and other needed supplies at the fort. The red men also could barter for white man's goods, using furs as the medium of exchange.

Chief Seattle came often to the fort and exchanged many furs for supplies. Dr. Tolmie knew the chief was a capable man, knew that he controlled the red men who resided on lands north of the fort, yet he did not approve of the chief. He warned Leschi against too close an association with Seattle. Leschi had become leader of the Nisqually tribe. He and Dr. Tolmie had formed a strong friendship.

The incident in the life of Seattle that alienated Dr. Tolmie seemed minor to the chief. One day when Seattle was gambling with some Duwamish Indians inside the fort he saw one of his tribesmen cheat in a game of chance. He knocked the Indian down. A fight developed and Seattle lashed out. Down went red men in every direction. When an official of the fort tried to intervene, Seattle knocked him down, too. Dr. Tolmie asked the Duwamish chief to leave the fort.

Seattle was gravely offended, but since Dr. Tolmie was chief at Fort Nisqually, Seattle left without comment. In a short while he returned with more furs, which he exchanged for a gun. He went outside and shot a member of his own tribe. Dr. Tolmie was shocked. He called Seattle a big brute with a black heart. But the chief of a tribe usually meted out justice to members of his tribe. Seattle ruled six tribes. He frequently was called upon to act as judge. He was renowned as a peaceful man, a fair and just man. Yet all red men on Puget Sound knew Seattle could be severe when he felt punishment was needed.

A man in a black robe arrived at Fort Nisqually soon afterward. He was Modeste Demers, a Catholic missionary, who'd volunteered to go to the far-off missions in the west where the white population was made up mostly of French-Canadian employees of the Hudson's Bay Company who desired a priest. Modeste Demers, in company with Father Blanchet, made the hazardous journey across the continent with scouts carrying supplies to the Hudson's Bay Company.

The journey from Quebec to Fort Vancouver, a distance of about five thousand miles, was made in canoes, by portage and barge, and on horseback. Upon reaching the Far West, Modeste Demers began to care for those he thought the most in need—the many Indian tribes who dwelt in the Oregon Territory.

When Father Demers reached Fort Nisqually, Dr. Tolmie opened the gates so that people could enter the grounds at will to listen to the services conducted by the priest. Indians who'd heard about the white man's religion quickly assembled to hear the man in the black robe. Many prominent Indian chiefs attended the services.

Among those who were present at all the meetings were Seattle, Leschi, and Quiemuth, brother of Leschi. Modeste Demers noticed the Indian leaders. He soon learned that they were men of superior intellect, so he spent many hours with them. He not only explained the concepts of the Christian religion, but also gave them a great deal of information about other races and other lands.

Many of the people who became Christians were baptized during the time the priest conducted the evangelistic services. He baptized Seattle, Leschi, Quiemuth, and other prominent chiefs on the same day. When he left the fort to go north, the chiefs who'd become Christians accompanied him. Indians heard of the man in the black robe who was traveling through the wilderness to tell red men about the strange religion. Audiences numbering from three hundred to three thousand people assembled to listen to the priest. More Indian chiefs joined

Father Demers. Several chiefs entered enemy territory, but they were safe. No one molested a chief who was following the man in the black robe.

Modeste Demers and Chief Seattle parted reluctantly when they reached the Strait of Juan de Fuca. The priest crossed the water to carry his message to tribes farther north. The chief returned home, determined to teach his tribesmen Christian principles and concepts. In accordance with these new Christian principles, Seattle freed all his slaves. He started daily religious classes at Old-Man-House. His tribes soon learned to repeat the Lord's Prayer in their respective dialects and in the Chinook jargon.

Shortly after Father Demers left Fort Nisqually, a Catholic mission was established on Puget Sound near what is now Olympia, and a Methodist mission was established near Fort Nisqually. The first missionaries went from settlement to settlement recalling faithful people to the practice of religion while explaining Christianity to the natives. As the years passed, missionaries established churches, schools and hospitals in the Oregon Territory.

# Chapter Twelve

## Ships with Wings

It was difficult for Indians to grasp the principles of personal property. Nature had always provided them with the necessities of life. They took what they wanted, whenever and wherever they found it, but never more than they needed or could use. But, as time went on, Seattle warned his tribesmen that they must obey the new laws of the white man.

"Your Father above says, 'Thou shalt not kill.' He will punish you if you kill white people or red people. And you must not steal from each other. If you steal the white man's goods, you will be punished."

Seattle also encouraged braves, who slept a large part of the day, to be more industrious. He urged them to hunt and trap and fish. "Furs buy white man's goods."

So his tribesmen went into the forest and canyons to hunt and fish. Whenever they were lucky, they shared food with all who were near.

It was on just such an occasion, when food was plentiful and the Suquamish were having hiyu muckamuck, an Indian jumped to his feet and pointed north. "Our enemies are coming. In big canoes with wings. They're flying over the water—the wings are moving!"

A medicine man jumped to his feet, waving his arms wildly. He picked up a club of driftwood. "Run for your lives!"

Pandemonium broke loose. Men picked up clubs as they ran to hide. Women shrieked, caught up their children, and ran into the woods. The children cried and screamed. Dogs barked and battled over the abandoned food.

Upon hearing the shouting, Seattle, who was in the potlatch house, came outside to see what was causing the disturbance. Pointing northward, the Indians talked excitedly. Seattle spoke quietly to the man nearest him. Both of them walked a short distance and stopped near some wood piled high on the beach. Seattle climbed to the top of the timbers to get a better view of the ships. He watched intently for a few minutes. Then his voice rang out.

"All of my tribesmen come close. I have something to say to you."

Even though they feared the monstrous ships, the Indians responded to his call. Seattle raised his arms, his usual signal for silence. His tribesmen looked apprehensively toward the north, but, somewhat calmed by the actions of their chief, sat on the seashore to listen.

"Don't be afraid," Seattle said. "Those ships are not the canoes of our northern enemies. They are like the *Beaver* canoe. They come from a faraway land. There are white men on those ships, and they are our friends. I've been expecting them for a long time."

He stopped talking for a few minutes. All eyes were focused on the vessels, which were approaching rapidly.

"Many seasons have passed since I, with Schweabe, my father, and Kitsap, our war chief, walked about on a ship like these." Seattle held up two fingers. "There were two ships, and they circled our shores many times. Kitsap was on one of them the entire time. When the ship sailed away, Kitsap returned to our tribe to tell us about the ships and about the white men on them. He told us that someday ships would again come to the Whulge.

"Now Schweabe, my father and builder of Tsu-Suc-Cub, has gone to a better place, leaving us here, now, to deal with what he knew and said would happen. Kitsap and I have seen the ships in visions many times, and now they are here. We'll watch them circle our shores without fear, for they are our friends."

With members of his tribe, Seattle quietly watched the ships pass by. They watched until the ships had disappeared beyond a point of land to the south.

The Indians again talked excitedly to one another. And, again, Seattle raised his arms. "The ships will sail to the end of the Whulge. Then they'll circle our shores perhaps several times before they sail away. They haven't come to fight or plunder. Watch them without fear."

Seattle stood still for a few minutes as if in deep thought. Then he turned around, walked back to the potlatch house and entered it. The Indians glanced apprehensively across the water from time to time as they resumed their usual activities.

A few days later, Seattle came from the potlatch house dressed in white man's clothes. He wore a shirt and pants with a Hudson's Bay blanket draped across his shoulders. He was followed by four of his tribesmen carrying some furs. They stepped into a canoe and paddled south. The Indians watched the canoe until it was out of sight.

The ships were the *Vincennes* and the *Porpoise* of the United States Navy. Their captain was Charles Wilkes, the great American explorer. He'd been sent by the United States government to chart Puget Sound and to explore the Oregon Territory. Besides the midshipmen and marines on the ships, there were scientists. There were surveyors with instruments and charts, botanists, mineralogists, taxidermists, and artists. The ships were bound for Fort Nisqually. They anchored at the mouth of the Nisqually River.

The Nisqually tribe, like the Suquamish Indians, were frightened. Like Kitsap, Leschi wasn't at home to reassure his tribesmen when the ships were sighted, so they ran into the forests to hide where they could peer through the underbrush and watch silently. The Indians saw fur traders leave the fort and missionaries leave the mission to walk to the water's edge. They saw officers from the ships come ashore in small boats. The officers were greeted cordially by the fur traders and the missionaries. When the peering eyes of the Indians saw the white people shaking hands, they became less fearful. They knew a handshake meant friendship. Gradually, they came from behind trees to tarry quietly near the mouth of the river or near the woods.

Men from the ships went ashore from time to time. Some of them entered the fort, while others entered the buildings of the Puget Sound Agricultural Company. In the eight years since its establishment, the company had built up a large agricultural and stock farm. There were hundreds of cattle grazing on pasturelands. There were seventy milk cows in the barns. The grain bins were filled. Wheat fields were green. Vegetables and berries were ready to harvest.

The Indians saw one man from the ships looking at vegetables through glasses. They saw another man climb a rocky cliff, pound with a small implement at the rock formation, then pick up some small pieces of rock and put them in his knapsack. They were further mystified to see a crew of men land and cut down trees with implements of steel. They saw building materials brought to shore, unloaded from the *Porpoise*.

"Are the men going to build another fort?" one Indian said.

Some men from the ship had unloaded a cannon. The Indians knew about small guns, which could be purchased at the Hudson's Bay trading post. The Nisqualies were procrastinators, but they were warriors. Apprehensively, they pondered about the significance of the big guns on the ships and the one on shore.

The Indians were so interested in the activities on land they failed to notice Seattle's canoe when it came alongside the *Vincennes*. But officers on the ship had seen the canoe through glasses when it left the shore and had been watching it as it drew near the mouth of the river.

The officers watched Seattle while he circled the ship three times. They saw him beach his canoe and enter one of the houses on the shore. Leschi, who'd just returned to Nisqually land wasn't surprised to see the chief. "I have been expecting you. I saw you circling the ships."

"You're watching the ships?" Seattle said.

"Yes, I'm watching everything. I'll fix food. We can talk while we eat," Leschi said. "I have met the chief of the boats. The white men from boats have looked at the fort, the farm, and the mission."

"What are they building?"

"Houses on land so they can explore our water, our land, our heavens."

"How can they explore the heavens from land?" Seattle said, perplexed.

"A trader at the post told me they explore the heavens through glasses. White men have many peculiar goods."

"We must welcome white men to our shores, for they know much," Seattle said. "We must learn from our white brothers and buy goods from them."

"How can we buy goods when we have few coins?"

"We don't need many coins. We have land. Once our people were many, but tribe fought tribe until now we are few. Red men no longer need extensive territory. White men want land and they have many goods. We can trade."

"We can trade. We have plenty of land for all men who want to raise food. Yes, white men are good traders. I traded horses at the farm. They gave me a plow with much metal. They gave me seed. I raise oats for my best ponies. I welcome white men to Nisqually land."

Leschi was silent for a few minutes. "The big chief of the ship has gone away through the forest to the big river. He left this morning. He has guides, and they're riding on ponies. The best pony belongs to me, and one of my scouts is riding him. My scout knows Chinook."

"That is well. We're friends of the white men, but we want to know what they're doing."

"They've gone to see white-headed Eagle."

White-headed Eagle, so named by the Indians, was Dr. John McLoughlin, the chief agent of the Hudson's Bay Company at Fort Vancouver. He was a tall, distinguished-looking man. In addition to being the chief agent at the fort, he was also superintendent of ali Hudson's Bay posts in the northwest. He was an extremely powerful man, for he governed the entire Oregon Territory.

Before leaving to visit Dr. McLoughlin, Captain Wilkes had established a base near the mouth of the Nisqually River. The structures being erected were an observatory and a house to be used by the scientists of his expedition. From this base, Commander Wilkes hoped to explore the Oregon Territory over land while sailors in small boats surveyed and charted Puget Sound.

Captain Wilkes visited all the trading posts and missions west of the Rocky Mountains. Scientists who gathered information about the almost impenetrable wilderness that was the great Oregon Territory accompanied him.

Meanwhile, Seattle stayed a few days on Nisqually land, then returned to Old-Man-House. As day after day passed, Seattle heard about the boats from the *Vincennes* that were sailing on the waterways of the Whulge, traveling up streams, going into harbors to anchor while the white men explored. The Indians watched them, but they did not fear the white men.

# Chapter Thirteen

# A Strange Celebration

Weeks passed before Seattle, accompanied by an interpreter, went again to Nisqually land. There, Seattle learned that Captain Wilkes had returned from his prolonged trip and that he intended to send the men from the ships ashore for a potlatch.

Chief Seattle's interpreter, like most Nisquallies, spoke Chinook. Englishmen were called "King George's Men," Americans were called "Bostons." The Bostons from the ship were coming ashore to potlatch with their friendly enemies, King George's Men.

Both groups of men liked horse racing, but they had no horses to race. Leschi had the most and best ponies on Nisqually land. The Bostons gave Leschi coins, who, in return, was to furnish ponies for the white men to race at the celebration.

The Indians watching from wooded areas, didn't know of the arrangements. They were puzzled when they saw Leschi put ponies in the corral of the agricultural company. They were more mystified when Leschi entered the fort, and other people who tried to enter, couldn't get inside. The gates were locked and Leschi was behind the stockade, a prisoner.

"Why are the gates locked? What is happening to Leschi?" Seattle wondered.

Fearfully, Indians watched the warships. The gates opened, and Leschi and two Bostons walked out of the stockade talking together. Leschi raised his hand and pointed toward the prairie where his horses were grazing. The Bostons nodded. Leschi then saw Seattle and motioned to him to join him and his companions. The four men talked for a few minutes, then Chief Seattle shook hands with the Bostons.

Leschi held up two fingers and pointed in the direction of his home. The gates of the corral opened and two horses were let out. Leschi whistled. The horses ran to the gates and stopped. Seattle mounted one. Leschi, a superb horseman, leaped onto the back of the other. Chief Seattle waved his hand as they galloped toward Leschi's farm.

After entering his farm home, Leschi told Seattle that the Bostons rented his horses so that they and King George's Men could have horse racing at their potlatch. "I put horses in the white man's corral. They gave me money. I will show you." Leschi displayed an assortment of money he'd received. The collection included two pieces of paper money, a dollar bill and a five-dollar bill.

Seattle examined the paper money carefully. "A missionary told me United States is a big country. It can make money out of paper. I have seen paper money buy much at the trading post. But why did King George's Men lock the gates while you were in the fort?"

"I asked Dr. Tolmie to lock gates while I made the bargain with the Bostons. I got more paper money, more coins. Leschi unwrapped a cloth that contained another five-dollar bill, another one-dollar bill, and two silver dollars, plus some smaller coins.

"What did the Bostons want?"

"Nothing. They want to see Nisqually Indians ride their own ponies at the potlatch. They give me big coins and paper money. I will make a big show for their potlatch. I will ride Lightning, my fastest pony. Nisqually scouts will ride my other fast ponies."

"Your best ponies are not in the white man's corral," Seattle said.

"No. I kept my best ponies, but the Nisqually want friendship with the white men. They gave me coins so I put other ponies in their corral. I want friendship with the chief of the big ship, so I traded with him, too. He gave me coins. He is a chief, so I gave him a good horse to ride on his trip. A good scout guided him, so now he's returned safely."

Sunday morning, at daylight, Leschi went out on the range to lasso his best horses. Seattle went to church at the Methodist mission, after which he spent the day talking with missionaries and fur traders.

Seattle learned that white-headed Eagle, upon hearing that the *Vincennes* and the *Porpoise* were anchored near Fort Nisqually, had ordered quantities of fresh food delivered to the ships. White-headed Eagle ordered the dairy at the farm to deliver fresh milk daily as long as the ships were in port.

Captain Wilkes, in turn, invited the chief agent of the Hudson's Bay Company to visit the United States warships while they were stationed at the isolated fort on Puget Sound. White-headed Eagle accepted the invitation, but had to send word that he was delayed on his trip north because of heavy rain and muddy trails.

"He won't arrive in time for the potlatch. Too bad," Seattle said.

"The men on those ships are Americans," a trader said. "Bostons is Chinook jargon. Americans of the United States Navy do not potlatch. Only Indians potlatch. Those Americans are coming ashore tomorrow to celebrate the Fourth of July on the fifth of July. Today is Sunday. The Americans don't celebrate on Sunday, so they'll celebrate the Fourth of July on Monday. Do you understand, chief?"

"No. What is a celebration."

"Don't try to understand," another trader said. "Just stick around until tomorrow and you will see a celebration when the United States Navy comes ashore."

Seattle knew the preparations for the celebration were being completed. Other red men were not so informed. With immense curiosity and uncertainty, they watched the preparatory activity. They saw a number of sailors come ashore and go to a lake situated about a mile from the observatory. The sailors dug a big pit and put a post at each end of it. They lifted a beam and put it on top of the posts. They erected tables in a grove of oak trees. Then they returned to the ships. Later the red men saw other sailors come with axes and ropes. They cut limbs from a fir tree as they climbed aloft. When they came down, a red, white, and blue piece of cloth was flying from the top of the tall tree. Later the sailors pulled the cloth down with ropes, but they left the ropes hanging on the tree. Then they pitched a tent under the tree and unloaded a gun and some blankets. Some sailors with big clubs strapped to their sides slept in the tent that night. When they awakened, the rope and the gun were in place, but the blankets had vanished.

When Seattle arrived to view the work, there would've been trouble had he heard of the theft. Captain Wilkes did not wish any sort of disruption of the celebration, so he ignored the theft of the blankets from the armed guards.

A slaughtered ox was suspended from the beam over the open pit.

"We'll turn it all night, and it'll roast through by tomorrow noon," a sailor said to a confused Seattle.

On Monday morning several hundred men in uniform were mustered on board the two ships at nine o'clock. The midshipmen and marines and band went ashore in small boats. Two howitzers were brought ashore. Upon landing, the midshipmen and marines formed ranks. The band began to play. Flags were unfurled and the men started marching in unison to the music. With flags flying, they marched to the lake a mile away. The Indians, fascinated, came from behind underbrush to follow the parade. The marching men were greeted with cheers and waving flags when they passed fur traders and missionaries. The excitement was so contagious that even the stoic red men cheered and waved.

When the marchers reached the lake, the cannons were fired in a salute that was answered by the guns at the fort. Startled, the Indians ran for cover. The uniformed men broke ranks and the festivities began. The band played the national anthem of both the United States and England. A chaplain led the audience in prayer. Reverend Dr. John P. Richmond, the minister who established the Methodist mission, delivered a patriotic oration.

Seattle and his interpreter listened to everything the minister said. Seattle heard every inflection of Reverend Richmond's voice, noticed every gesture, and noted audience reaction to all that was said. At the end of the oration, the men in uniform took off their hats and waved them. Captain Wilkes, in full dress uniform, led a procession to the picnic tables under the trees. A gong sounded.

The sailors ran to their allotted places in the grove while the officers and their guests walked to the tables that had been erected under the oak trees. The Indians had been directed to remain quietly at a distance until the white people finished. They were told they could have all the food that remained on the tables.

The hungry red men smelled the white man's food as they watched and waited. A long period of time elapsed before the white people left the tables. Immediately, the red men ran across the grass to the tables, grabbed the food, and devoured it. They were able to eat until they could consume no more.

Seattle watched from a distance. He pitied his people. They were so ignorant and so helpless. They had so little, and they needed so much, and they were so hungry for the white man's bread. He walked over to the grove and joined his people.

Seattle called his interpreter and talked with him for a few minutes. Then, with the interpreter carrying the skin of a beaver, Seattle approached an officer.

"Our chief wants to present a gift to your commander. Can you take it to him?" The interpreter said.

"Perhaps I can. What does he wish to give Captain Wilkes?" The officer said.

"The chief wants to give your commander the skin of a beaver. He says to tell him that it's a gift of friendship from the

Indian chiefs of Puget Sound, who welcome both the great American explorer and the United States Navy to our waters."

The officer was astonished but he accepted the gift. "In the name of our commander, I accept with pleasure a present from the chiefs of Puget Sound."

Seattle put the fur in one hand of the officer, shook the other hand vigorously, turned, and walked away.

The afternoon program started at two o'clock. By the time Seattle arrived at the festival grounds, men in uniform, Indians, fur traders, missionaries, and settlers were already assembled to watch the sports events. He witnessed a strange spectacle. Men in uniform of the Navy were racing Indian ponies, while the Indians who owned the ponies were on the sidelines cheering and betting extravagantly.

As the grand finale of the afternoon, Leschi, Quiemuth, and other Nisqually horsemen rode onto the field. They put on a show never to be forgotten. The riders stood on the backs of the ponies, rode under them, and over them. They fell off the ponies and jumped on them again. They howled like wolves and shouted war cries. The ponies stood up on their hind legs. They galloped, turned, twisted, rolled over, but somehow most of the Nisquallies stayed on their mounts.

Thus the celebration ashore ended. It had been a glorious day for everyone. The sailors ran on good solid earth. They ate food deliciously prepared. The courageous missionaries and fur traders, who lived and worked in an isolated place in the wilderness, were overjoyed to see friends from far away. The Indians enjoyed the pageantry of the parade, the excitement of the races, and the display of horsemanship. They enjoyed a feast such as they'd never had.

There was more celebration to come. When darkness came, a gun was fired at sea, whereupon thousands of falling stars dropped from the sky. The fireworks continued for a short time.

The officer who'd received the beaver skin didn't have an opportunity to give it to his commander until after the display of shooting stars.

"Did you find out anything about the chief who sent the message to me?" the captain said.

"Indeed I did, Sir. The fur traders know him. He's the biggest Indian chief on Puget Sound. A powerful man, they say."

"I saw that Indian," a man said. "He must be over six feet tall. I'll warrant he's as strong as an ox, built like an athlete."

Another man, a taxidermist, joined the group.

"What about this beaver skin? Is it a good specimen?" Captain Wilkes said.

"It's the best specimen I've ever seen," the taxidermist said.

"You'll be able to use it?" The captain said.

"Indeed, we will," the taxidermist replied.


On July sixth, Captain Wilkes was relieved to learn that Dr. McLoughlin had arrived safely at the fort. The captain invited Dr. McLoughlin to lunch with him at the observatory and later to go aboard the *Vincennes* to inspect the warship. The tour of the ship ended in the captain's private quarters, where the two men discussed the problem that was disturbing England and the United States at that time: where in the vast, unsurveyed wilderness was the line that divided the United States and Canada? Captain Charles Wilkes, the explorer who'd discovered the Antarctic, and Dr. Charles McLoughlin, who controlled the fur-trading empire west of the Rocky Mountains, didn't know where the line should be placed. By treaty in 1846, the line between the United States and Canada was established at the 49th parallel. Puget Sound was in the northwestern corner of the United States. Nootka, the trading post established by Spain, was in Canada. Old-Man-House, which was erected on land owned by the Indians for centuries, was in the United States.

Forts Vancouver and Nisqually, owned by a British firm, were on American soil.

An agent at Nisqually tried to explain the conditions of the treaty to both Seattle and Leschi. He spread out a map. "See this line? All land north of the line belongs to King George's Men, and all land south of the line belongs to the Bostons. Do you understand?"

Although Seattle could neither read nor write, he could interpret the map. "Yes, we understand. All Indians on the Whulge are American Indians. Our enemies to the north, the Nootkas, the Tsimshian, the Haidas are still our enemies. They will not see a line on water. They will go right through it in their big war canoes."

"If our enemies attack, we will fight," Leschi said.

"We will not fight them," Seattle said. "I have the power of the luminous sea gull. I have visions of things to come." Seattle looked intently at the fur trader. "Do white men ever have visions?" he asked.

## Chapter Fourteen

## Visions of White Men

Like Chief Seattle, white men also had visions. In the eighteen forties, men with visions of a rainbow at the end of a long journey, set out for the west with its homesteading opportunities. When the weary occupants of the long, slow-moving wagon trains finally reached the Columbia River, they knew they were near Fort Vancouver, a stopping place on the way to their ultimate destination, the Williamette River valley.

A few pioneers, however, traveled north over old Indian trails to stake claims to land on small prairies near the banks of rivers. Upon those rivers the homesteaders could travel by canoe to trading posts for supplies and mail.

A trading post established on the Cowlitz River, named Cowlitz Landing, became a well-known stopping place for both fur traders and pioneers. Fur traders went farther north along an old trail to the southern shores of Puget Sound, but the progress of the new settlers was stopped by swamps on the lowland between Cowlitz Landing and the Sound.

Among the early pioneers with vision was Michael Simmons. He and members of his party were the first to take donation claims on the shores of Puget Sound. Like many other settlers, he went first to the Williamette Valley. He didn't find a homestead that suited him, so he decided to investigate the Puget Sound area. He went by canoe to Cowlitz Landing, then along the Indian trail until he reached a place the Indians called Tum Chuck. There, the De Chutes River emptied into the Sound in a cascade of falls eighty feet high. Simmons realized the falls could produce power, and he wanted to build a mill. Then, when he saw the Nisqually trading post and the farm of the agricultural company, he knew he'd found his rainbow. He went south to get

.

his family. While there, he persuaded some friends to go with him to Puget Sound.

"There's endless forests, but also there's prairies in river valleys," Simmons said. "And there's the best trading post in the northwest. But travel beyond Cowlitz Landing is difficult. There's no road over which a wagon could travel. I studied the trail on my return trip and I know it can be widened to the north clear through to the falls, where I staked my claim. If everyone would help, we could get wagons through the swamps between the Cowlitz and Puget Sound and you could all stake homesteads there."

On one of his trips to Fort Nisqually, Seattle learned that the white men were opening a road from the big river to the Whulge, a road over which covered wagons and livestock were traveling. Although from his earliest childhood Seattle had visions of gigantic ships sailing into the Whulge and visions of red and white men dwelling on the shores of those inland waterways, he hadn't thought of whites coming to his lands in covered wagons. Seattle was not disturbed. He believed there was enough land along the shores of the Whulge for both Indians and whites. When he received word that settlers with women and children were on their way to the Whulge, he went at once to see Leschi.

"I know they're coming," Leschi said. "Women with children are driving cows. Men are cutting trees with metal tools, putting wagons on sleds to get through the swamps."

"We must help them."

"Help them? How? Why?"

"We want white men to live on our shores so we can learn their way of life. Help them and we help ourselves. We must welcome them, for we have much land and their God is now our God. If they come to live with us, we will someday have clothes to wear and white man's food to eat," Seattle said.

"Metal tools I want to cultivate land, but we have few furs to trade for goods."

"We have land covered with trees, land for all, so I'm going to meet them at the far end of the Whulge to welcome them to our lands, and you must welcome them to Nisqually shores."

"I'll tell Dr. Tolmie that white men are coming in wagons," Leschi said. "I'll say I'm the son of a Nisqually chief, so I'll welcome them. I'll say that the chief of Duwamish and some of his tribesmen will be at Tum Chuck to welcome the whites to our Whulge."

"That will be well. My men will be camping near Tum Chuck when they arrive."

"I'll watch the Nisqually braves, for they have the spirit of war," Leschi said. "I'll keep them peaceful."

Later, when Simmons returned to the falls with his family, he was astonished to find a large number of Indians camping on the land he had staked for a homestead. An Indian came forward and offered to shake hands. Simmons was relieved to learn the natives were friendly. People traveling in the wagon trains always feared attack by unfriendly natives.

A little later, Simmons was even more surprised when two men approached the area where he was establishing a camp. One of them was a white man, the other appeared to be an Indian chief.

"I've come from the fort to act as an interpreter for Chief Seattle," the white man said. "He's the chief of the tribes who live to the north. He also speaks for Chief Leschi, who is the leader of the Indians on these shores. Chief Seattle will talk with you." The interpreter turned toward the chief and bowed his head.

Seattle acknowledged the introduction, then bowed to others of the party who'd come from a tent. All stood perfectly still while Seattle spoke in a low, clear voice. "We canoe Indians want peace with white men. We want to do business with you. We have endless country, so we welcome you to our shores. I am chief of the Duwamish and Suquamish tribes. I will, if you wish, take you farther north in canoes to explore the lands of my people." He bowed to Mr. Simmons.

Simmons thanked the chief. "I've been farther north in a canoe, beyond Fort Nisqually. I've been south beyond the Columbia River. We want to stay with our women and children here, where I've staked a claim. That's why we widened the trail to make a road to these falls."

Seattle bowed and glanced around the camp. "Did you use metal tools to cut the road through the forest?"

"We used axes, sledges, and saws."

"I'd like to see them."

"Of course. Come this way."

Curious natives watched Seattle carefully examine the tools, tools made of metal.

"Was it hard to cut a road through the woods?" the chief said.

"It was, but we've had hard travel before. We come two thousand miles over the Oregon Trail, and that was mighty hard work. We knew when we left Cowlitz Landing we wasn't going on no picnic. Many times we had to cut our way through the woods, but we got through. We're here now."

"You haven't told the chief that on the Oregon Trail we never had to get around enormous stumps nor build a road over decayed trees that had fallen in the pathway," Edmond Sylvester, another member of the Simmons party, said.

"No. I didn't say nothin' about that because the worst thing we had was that everlastin' rain. By workin' hard we could do 'most anything with our tools, but we couldn't do a thing about rain."

Seattle laughed and spoke to the interpreter. "Tell him my tribesmen rest under trees when it rains, and wait for rain to stop."

"Our livestock, like your men, ran for shelter under the trees, and our women had an awful time with them," Simmons said.

"Not as bad a time as you had," Sylvester said. "Our wagons mired in swampy holes, and you should've seen Mike trying to pull us through that mud."

"Well, I wallowed us through it all right to the end of this long trail. So you can see how it is, chief. I reckon I'll stay right here where I've already staked my claim. I hope you won't object to me building a grist mill where the falls 'll give me power to run it."

"What is a grist mill?" the chief said.

"A grist mill grinds grain into flour so women can bake bread. I had a grist mill in Kentucky where I come from," Simmons said.

"That's good. Leschi will like a gristmill on Nisqually land. He raises grain on his farm near the fort, and he wants bread for his people. I'll stop at Leschi's farm to tell him whites want to build homes on our Whulge. I'll tell him you'll grind his grain with power from the falls. I mean when you build—what did you call it?"

"A grist mill."

Before returning to Old-Man-House, Seattle talked to his people. He assured them that whites camping near the falls were friends. He stated emphatically that severe punishment would follow theft. After Seattle's departure, a subchief presented Simmons with deer meat and salmon to express friendship. Shortly thereafter, red people and white people were on the beach together, gathering oysters. Squaws showed white women how to cook the oysters. The friendly natives camped near the settlers. With great interest they watched the whites build homes. Each group learned much from the other.

Michael Simmons established the first town on Puget Sound. He gave it an Indian name, Tumwater, which in Chinook, meant, "falling water." He built the first gristmill on the Sound using hand-hewn cedar plank. The wheat was ground between granite boulders cut from native stone. Pioneer women made bread and muffins from the ground wheat and corn.

Simmons also built the first saw mill on the Sound. The mill couldn't manufacture finished lumber, but with the second-hand machinery purchased from the Hudson's Bay Company, wide planks two inches thick at one end and four inches thick at the other, were cut. The earliest settlers used the planks extensively for the construction of the first buildings.

Members of the Simmons party wanted to build homes near one another, but the donation act provided that each man with a wife could get a homestead title to 640 acres of land, but he must live on the land for five years. So the houses were necessarily far apart.

One member of the Simmons' party, McAllister, paddled up a stream in a canoe until eventually he saw Fort Nisqually. While inspecting the farm of the Puget Sound Agricultural Company he, by chance, met a friendly Indian who spoke English. Both had stopped to watch some men at work on a new structure on the farm.

"You must be one of the men who cut the trail so that oxen and horses can be driven to our waters," the Indian said.

"I am. We knew the only trading post on Puget Sound was here, but we didn't expect to find so large a settlement, nor did we expect to find a beautiful prairie surrounded by such magnificent scenery."

The Indian pointed to Tahoma. "The mountain is a god like our Father in the sky. Do you like our Tahoma?"

"I sure do. It's the most beautiful mountain I've ever seen."

"We have much land, few Nisquallies. Plenty of land for white men to—what do you call it? I know, stake a homestead. Come with me. I'll show you more land."

McAllister followed the Indian to some grazing land.

"My horses. You take this one," the Indian said.

McAllister mounted the horse and followed the Indian. They passed some cultivated land. "My farm and my brother's farm," the Indian said. "Nisqually land is good land. Raises big crops. I'll show you."

The Indian guided McAllister across a pasture to a place where two mountain streams met to form a larger stream. "This is good place for you. Good land, plenty of water. You like it?"

"It's unbelievable. Is there some way I can stake out a homestead here? I could build a mill here."

"Nisqually chief will give you the land."

"What makes you think the chief will let me settle here?"

"We want white friends to settle on Nisqually lands. We want to trade for metal. We want to trade for clothes and for bread. The chief is old. I'm his son, Leschi. I'm leader of our tribe now. You can have this land."

It was the chance meeting with Leschi that made it possible for McAllister to secure a homestead with fertile soil at a place where two streams met. He set to work at once to build living quarters for his wife and five children. There were two huge hollow stumps on his new homestead. He cleaned out the inside of the stumps and put a roof on each. There he and his family lived until, with the aid of Indians, he completed a log house.

He built a sawmill at the fork of the river. McAllister formed friendships with all the Indians who worked for him. He was taken into the Nisqually tribe, and he and his family lived according to Nisqually laws. Mrs. McAllister hired squaws to help with household duties and to care for her children.

At first the McAllisters were dismayed when they learned their home was near the Nisqually tribal grounds, but they soon became accustomed to shrieking warriors. The McAllister children learned the meaning of the signals, the wolf howls and owl hoots. They learned to chant like Indians, learned their battle songs. They even came to know the meaning of the death howl. The white children and the native children played together happily.

Edmond Sylvester, the other member of the Simmons party, was neither interested in agriculture nor was he interested in a mill, but he had visions, too. He wanted to go into business. He built a town two miles north of the falls so ocean vessels could anchor in the harbor. He erected two or three cabins, a two-story building, and established a store. He named the town Olympia.

Duwamish Indians, who were camping when the Simmons party arrived at the falls, decided to help Sylvester build his town. They erected a few small plank huts on the Sylvester homestead not far from his store. Other Indians lived along the beach in winter houses built of driftwood.


Chief Seattle visited his tribes frequently. The visits provided him with the opportunity to watch the progress of the pioneers. He was fascinated by their ways. Their ingenuity and industriousness intrigued him. The rapidity with which their new way of living was established mystified Seattle. "The ways of the whites are good. Quickly they build storm-proof homes. Quickly they make the land ready for planting. Men help the white squaws, not like our men, who fish and hunt only when they're hungry. When light comes over Tahoma, whites start to work and they work steadily until the sun lowers itself in water. Only on the Sabbath do they rest. Why don't my tribesmen work hard? Our people have lived on these lands for generations past. Our ways remain the same. We must change. We must watch our white brothers to learn from them."

Seattle became one of the first customers at the new store. He, accompanied by several subchiefs, walked into the store and displayed a large number of beaver skins. "In the past I met traders at Nisqually, but henceforth I trade at your store. You will take beaver skins for coins?"

Beaver skins, as well as other furs, were the media of exchange in Oregon Territory, so Sylvester gladly accepted the furs. Thereafter, Chief Seattle and his tribesmen seldom went to Nisqually to trade. Instead, they traded at the new trading post in Olympia.

In 1845, shortly after the Simmons party cut the road from Cowlitz Landing to Puget Sound, a great migration northward began. Olympia became an important settlement because ships could unload the supplies needed by pioneer families and could load logs destined for the San Francisco market.

# Chapter Fifteen

# The White Medicine Man

When Chief Seattle heard that some whites were coming by boat to settle on land across the Whulge from Tsu-Suc-Cub, he sent a scouting party. "I've been watching and waiting many moons for the white man to come to our lands," Seattle thought. "I wish to welcome the white man, for my people can learn much from him. We need metal tools to plow our land and bring forth food. Newcomers will build strong houses. With tools, my men can build sturdy houses. "Newcomers to our lands have many clothes, warm clothes. My men, women, and children need warm clothes to fight off the wind and rain. Too many Indians die from cold and hunger. Even I need white man's medicine and a white medicine man. My bones hurt. With each passing year, my hands become more clumsy.

"White man will teach us. We must help him, watch him, and learn from him. I will go to Duwamish lands to welcome the strangers when they set foot on our soil. I go to tell the strangers I am their friend. I will tell them that red man can teach whites, too; that we can live together in peace. Is not my guardian spirit the luminous sea gull?"

A large number of Indians watched the members of the Denny party land on Duwamish shore. David Denny had preceded the main party, and, in anticipation of their coming, had built a crude shelter.

As the party landed, David came from his tent to greet the newcomers. "Don't fear the Indians camping near here. They're friendly. I hurt my foot and they treated me well. They built fires for me and brought food. They've been kind to me."

Later, one of the Indians, who'd watched the group come ashore approached the camp accompanied by a chief. "I am Chief Seattle's mouth. He wishes to give you a message."

The interpreter bowed to his chief; and the chief returned the bow. "Chief Seattle is the chief of the Suquamish Tribe and the big tyee of the Duwamish Federation of Tribes. You are now on his land. He wishes to speak to you."

"I've been expecting you for an endless time," Seattle said. "Now I can welcome you to the shores of my ancestors. You're our pioneer brothers. We have extensive territory, plenty for white and red men. When other ships come into our waters, we will welcome them, too. We wish to trade with the white man. People from my tribes will come to show you the trails through the forest, to take you places in canoes so you can procure food for your people."

Then, with great dignity, the chief shook hands with all the men and departed. Soon some Indians came from the forest and placed salmon and smoked deer meat in front of the camp of the settlers. The pioneers were scarcely over their surprise when other Indians began to make camp in the area nearby. One thousand of them—men, women, and children—arrived eventually to remain all winter.

The people of two markedly different cultures lived peacefully side-by-side during the winter. As Chief Seattle had foretold, the Indians helped the whites during that first winter. Both groups learned to adjust. The settlers grew accustomed to the glare of inquisitive eyes. Squaws and braves entered cabins at will, peered through doors and windows. Living a communal life for generations, the Indians had no understanding of personal property. When hungry, the Indian entered a pioneer home to take bread from the table. Whatever attracted him, he took.

The Indian, however, had acquired some of white man's civilization from their association with fur traders, missionaries, and the first white people who settled near Olympia. Some braves spoke the Chinook jargon, a few spoke English well enough to converse with the whites. Many of the pioneers soon learned the Chinook jargon, a dialect of about 300 words.

Chief Seattle sensed the principles by which the white man lived. He cautioned his tribesmen against taking the white man's belongings, saying white men considered it wrong to take the possessions of another. White men called such actions stealing and punished a person caught with another's goods. Seattle warned his warriors that he, too, would punish a tribesman who took white man's belongings.

The new settlers realized that Chief Seattle was a powerful man, that he had a great deal of knowledge and understanding, that his word was law in his tribes, and that he exerted influence over other chiefs.

One day Seattle visited the men of the Denny party. He'd brought the chief of the Snoqualmies, Pat Kanim, with him. On this occasion Pat Kanim was his interpreter, for the Snoqualmie chief spoke English. Seattle never learned English nor did he ever use Chinook jargon.

"My tribes will not make war on your people," Pat Kanim said. "Like my great friend, the noble chief of the Duwamish Federation of Tribes, I and my people will aid you who are building homes upon our lands. We wish to be your friends and to learn from you as we teach you to fish, hunt, and explore these rivers, mountains, and valleys."

The winter days were filled with sights interesting to the Indians. Squaws in wonderment watched white women hang clothes out to dry, clothes so different from their own. Squaws peered through windows and doors of the newly constructed cabins. They'd giggle and chatter when a pioneer woman filled a tub with water and bathed her child.

Braves followed inquisitively the activity of the new settlers. They helped the settlers build cabins. They helped clear land for the plow.

Companionships continued to develop. There was work to be done, and the Indians were glad to work for white man's goods. The white men contracted with the captain of a brig, the *Leonesa*, to cut timbers for the San Francisco market. With

Indian help, the contract was fulfilled. Thus began the lumber industry of the Pacific Northwest.

Word was brought to Chief Seattle that a white medicine man had come to Olympia, the new settlement on Puyallup land. Seattle journeyed to the new outpost of civilization to talk with the white man's doctor. Seattle found that the man he sought had established a store and medical office.

His interpreter pointed to the sign above the door, which read "David Maynard, M.D." As they entered the store, the interpreter said, "Are you the white medicine man?"

"That I am. What can I do for you?" the doctor said.

"The chief wants to know how a white medicine man makes a sick man well."

"Well, it depends on the nature of his illness. Usually, I put a patient to bed, cover him so he'll keep warm and give him some medicine. Almost always the sick man recovers."

The doctor pulled a bench from behind the counter. "Sit down on this bench and be comfortable while we talk. I don't have any customers coming in today."

The chief and the doctor talked for a long time. The chief learned a great deal about white medicine men. He was mystified to learn the doctor could repair broken arms and legs, and that he could cure a toothache.

The doctor told the chief about his trip west, describing the country he'd traversed. "Our wagon train had traveled only a short distance when cholera struck. For a distance of one thousand miles along the Platte River, I took care of the sick. So many men died of cholera that some wagons were without drivers, so I drove a wagon clear through to Tumwater. I wanted to start a new life, but I didn't know what to do or where to go. I saw a road through the woods and followed it. I reached Olympia. And, after traveling over hundreds of miles of dry desert land, the inland waterway you call the Whulge looked good to me. I knew there weren't enough people to support a doctor, so I decided to become both a doctor and a merchant."

The chief listened intently.

"To become a merchant I needed goods to sell. I hired some Indians. We cut shakes and cord wood, then loaded the timbers on a schooner. I took them to San Francisco. I got a good price for the load. A ship had wrecked in the Bay. I bought her cargo. That's the way I got the merchandise that I'm selling."

The chief described his potlatch house, Tsu-Suc-Cub. He described the Whulge, Suquamish and Duwamish land, the way his people procured their food, the way they lived. He told of the warriors who lived across the Strait of Juan de Fuca and of the hostile warriors east of the Cascade Mountains. "My people are friendly toward white people. I am chief of many tribes. We have endless land. We've welcomed white settlers to our shores. We live in peace with them."

Some customers entered the store. The chief, preparing to leave, held out his hand. "We are friends."

"We are, indeed," Dr. Maynard said.

The chief left the store only to return a little later. "I'm coming again with a canoe to take you to see my home. I want to show you my Duwamish lands. There, on Duwamish land, you can meet some of your own tribesmen."

"I'd enjoy that. Eventually, I may settle farther north."

"You want to move to Duwamish lands?" Seattle said.

"No. I'd have no place to put my merchandise and no way of moving it. But come visit me again and I'll go with you to see your land and my tribesmen who have settled there. It's just possible I may some day settle there myself."

"I will come," the chief said as he left the store to return to Tsu-Suc-Cub.

Several weeks later, the doctor watched Chief Seattle beach three canoes and a barge. The chief and his interpreter came directly into the store.

"I've come to move your goods," Seattle said.

"You've what?" the astonished doctor said.

"I've talked to subchiefs of my tribe. All of them want a white medicine man. All of them want a store. Mr. Denny, your tribesman, is going to build a big town on Duwamish land. Two ships have come to our shores since I was here. White men went into the woods to cut timbers for the new town of San Francisco.

"I think if San Francisco wants lumber, it will want fish. I see visions of many ships sailing into our waters. I have visions of my tribes cutting timbers, of my fishermen catching plenty of salmon. I want a store where my people can buy white man's goods. I want a white medicine man. My tribesmen will help you build a store on Duwamish land, and I'll give you the land."

Chief Seattle pointed toward the barge and the canoes. "I'll move you."

The doctor sat in stunned silence as he listened to the interpreter repeat everything the chief said. "I'm speechless. Did you know the chief was making preparations for me to move?"

"Yes, I've known about it. I'm his interpreter. Everything has been arranged."

The doctor studied the chief intently for a minute. "You've had a long journey, so you must be tired. I'm a doctor. I'm going to fix something for you."

Dr. Maynard took a teakettle from a shelf, opened the door, and went into the backyard to a stone fireplace. He filled the teakettle from a small wooden trough through which ran clear fresh water. Then he put the kettle on the grate and started a fire. When the water boiled, the doctor put some tea leaves in it. He then returned to the store and put a generous amount of brown sugar into the tea.

He poured the sweetened liquid into cups and handed them to the visitors. "Drink this slowly while I prepare some food. We'll rest while we eat, and then we'll talk some more."

Dr. Maynard opened a cupboard from which he took a kettle that contained cold boiled beans seasoned with salt pork. Before going outdoors again, he poured the rest of the sweetened tea into the cups. He then put the beans to heat on the grate. He prepared another pot of hot tea. On the counter in the store he placed dishes for three people, a large loaf of bread, some dried applesauce, and a jug of molasses. The Indians continued to sip the sweetened tea while they watched the preparation of the meal.

"Pull your bench up to the counter and we'll eat," the doctor said. "Then you can tell me how you can manage to move that barge when it's loaded with merchandise."

"These are our best canoes. The men are our best paddlers. We'll move your goods through the swift waters in the canoes."

"Through the swift waters in the canoes," repeated the bewildered doctor. "Where are the swift waters?"

"Between two shores where the Whulge is narrow. Our canoes will move your white man's goods through the swift waters safely."

Ten days later, the doctor bade his friends in Olympia and Tumwater farewell and was on his way north to the Duwamish lands.

# Chapter Sixteen

## Metropolis of the Northwest

When Chief Seattle and his tribesmen beached the loaded barge and canoes, they saw white men standing on the shore.

Dr. Maynard stepped ashore and approached the men. "Name's Maynard."

"Glad to meet you, Maynard. My name's Arthur Denny. This is my brother David. And these men are Boren and Bell."

The men shook hands.

"I've been expecting to meet you," Maynard said. "Chief Seattle has told me about you and about the new town you're building."

"What in the world does the chief have on that barge and in those canoes?" David said.

"That stuff belongs to me," the doctor said. "I've been operating a store in Olympia. Chief Seattle and I have become friends. He suggested we go into business together. He expects a large run of salmon any time. His tribesmen are fishermen, and he wants a market for their fish, so he persuaded me to come to where there's lowland for fishermen to beach canoes full of salmon, a place where we can salt the salmon before sending it to San Francisco. So here we are."

"I never thought of the fish industry," David said. "We've just sent a load of logs to San Francisco. Timber's in great demand, but fish, I just don't know."

"I know the demand for timber is great," the doctor said. "When I first reached the Sound, I hired Indians to help me cut cordwood and shakes. As good fortune would have it, I turned that load into the merchandise you see on the barge. Chief's a great fellow. He's looking for a place to unload my goods now. His people want to trade fish for supplies. Wish me luck. I'm not a fisherman. I ran a store only a short time in Olympia. I've been a doctor for many years."

"You're a doctor?"

"I started west intent on changing my occupation, but cholera swept through our wagon train, so I set to work doctoring the sick. Ever since I reached the Sound I've been doctoring settlers and Duwamish Indians."

"This is unexpected good luck," David said.

The doctor glanced at the encampment of Indians. "Well, I guess I can always find sickness wherever I go. I think I'll find customers as well."

"We're going to build a city," Arthur said. "You'd better see our new harbor. Look the whole place over. We can go there by canoe in the morning. If you'll come to my cabin, I'll show you a map I made of the area."

"Look at that crowd of Indians," David said anxiously. "Aren't they pushing your merchandise out to sea again?"

The doctor climbed on a stump to look out over the water. "Yes. They've launched the barge and the canoes, probably to take them to some place of safety. I see the chief is commanding the expedition." He stepped to the ground. "I'd like to see your map."

The next day Arthur Denny, Boren, Bell, Maynard, and the Indian chief with his interpreter stood on the shore bordering the newly discovered deep-sea harbor.

"We haven't had time to go to Oregon City to record our claims, so we can easily change our lines to give you a good location to conduct business," Arthur said.

"That's really asking a great deal of you," Dr, Maynard said.

"Not at all." Boren pointed to the map of the survey Arthur had made. "If Bell moves his line a little this way, I can move mine to give you three hundred feet of waterfront. We can stake our claims to these homesteads and establish a business district."

Maynard turned to the interpreter. "Ask the chief to look at this map." He explained the proposal to Chief Seattle.

The chief nodded.

The lines were moved, and the men soon went to work on their claims. But the lines had to be moved again to accommodate another man, Henry Yesler, who was seeking a location for a lumber mill. All agreed that a mill would be a great asset.

A year later, New York Alki became a small town. Yesler's mill was run by steam, the first steam mill on Puget Sound. Yesler built a large cook and mess house, which also served as a community center. Ocean vessels were able to land at Yesler's dock. A skid road extended into the woods for oxen to pull logs to the water.

Maynard erected a building for a store. The building, twenty-six feet by eighteen feet, had a shake roof. An attic room with windows extending across the front became the doctor's living quarters. Soon an addition to the building was used as a drug store and a doctor's office.

The log houses of the first settlers were located in the woods surrounding the business area. Newly arrived settlers, whose homes were built in the river valleys nearby, purchased supplies at the Maynard store. And they sought his professional services when illness struck.

One day, some pioneers chanced to meet the doctor on the street near his store. "What came in on that British ship that just docked?" one of the men said.

"Some second-hand clothes and some scrap iron to trade to the Indians for furs, an order of supplies for my store, and a crew of loggers to help the Indians cut piles and shakes. The captain has a large order for timbers for the San Francisco market."

"That means New York Alki 'll become a lumber metropolis. San Francisco wants lumber and we've got the trees," one man said.

"It'll never be a metropolis unless we change its name."

"It's a strange name, but what else can we name our town? Those towns in California have Spanish names. We'll have to name it 'Sans—something', or 'San Tee something'," another man said.

"Why not call it Cascade, after the mountains?"

"I've heard people call this place Suquamps or Duwamps," someone said.

"That's it, we'll give this lumber metropolis an Indian name. We'll name it 'Seattle' after our chief. He not only gave us the land, he gave us the friendship of all the Indian tribes he controls," said the doctor.

After very little discussion, the founders of the city-to-be agreed unanimously to name the new town after the generous, friendly chief. The name became official in 1853 when the town was platted, after Washington Territory was established with Olympia as the territorial capital. President Pierce appointed Major Isaac Ingalls Stevens, born in Massachusetts, a graduate of West Point, as governor of the new territory.

# Chapter Seventeen

# A New Trail

When Governor Stevens arrived in Olympia, the town was the largest in the territory. Olympia was a bustling frontier town. It had a central square, a business district, and a number of dwellings for Indians and whites. There was a wharf where ocean vessels could load and unload freight. The population numbered about three hundred white people and approximately the same number of Indians.

Many of the whites that lived on Puget Sound came on sailing vessels. The opportunity for employment in mills and logging camps attracted them to the far northwest territory. Some of the earliest pioneers, after having traveled over the Oregon Trail, journeyed north from the Columbia River over the mud road the Simmons party had traveled. Progress over the mud road was exceedingly difficult and hazardous.

So settlers in Olympia were elated when they learned twenty-two thousand dollars had been allotted by the government for a military road through Naches Pass over the Cascade Mountains. Such a road would provide a safer route to their area.

When they learned that the promised funds were not available, after all, some enterprising citizens decided to build their own road. They took up a collection and raised two thousand dollars. Pioneers agreed to donate labor, so thirty-five men left at once to slash a wagon road over the pass. Pack horses carrying tools and food accompanied them.

It soon became evident that there was a shortage of horses.

The foreman sought help from Chief Leschi. "We're working on the Naches Pass road and we just ain't got enough horses to get supplies in and things moved around. Men working on the road brought in some horses, but we need at least twelve more. We're anxious to get the road done so them caravans on the Oregon Trail can get through the mountains this fall. I've been wonderin' if you'll rent us some horses."

"I have horses to rent. Twelve, yes," Leschi said.

The foreman took his moneybag from his pocket. "What'll it cost?"

"How much do white men get for their horses?"

"Oh, nothing. They just brought in the tools and the food on the pack horses when they started to work and so they just kept on using them."

"If white men get pay for horses, I get pay for my horses. Same pay."

"Well, white men don't get nothing."

"If white men use their horses to get work done quick, I'll send horses. Nisqually, Puyallups, and Muckleshoots want the road through the pass. The Yakimas want a road too so they can cross with women and children to camp and fish. My brother, Quiemuth, is the best guide to build a road, and he wants a road. He will come with horses and he'll tell you best way through mountains."

The foreman held out his hand. "Thanks, Leschi. I'm sure glad the Indians want a road, and I hope they'll use it when it's done."

Leschi shook hands with the foreman and smiled. "We'll use it, same as the white man."

The two men parted. The foreman went back into the wilderness and Leschi went out on the range to lasso the horses.

The previous spring a long wagon train had left Independence, Missouri bound for the Pacific Northwest. Those traveling in the caravan listened intently to their leader as he talked enthusiastically about the magnificent future of Puget Sound, which he said could be reached by going through a new pass in the Cascade Mountains. The immigrants were happy to learn that it would be possible for them to travel through the pass and avoid both the hazards of a trip through the Columbia River gorge and the swamps of the mud road.

After crossing the Blue Mountains, a caravan of thirty wagons and one hundred forty people left the Oregon Trail at Pendleton. They cut their way through matted clumps of sage brush only to find when they reached the Cascades there was no road other than an Indian trail. The leader was perplexed. "I just can't understand it. The last report I had, fifty men were working on the road. Why isn't it through by now?"

"We cant go back. Whatever 'll we do?" the weary travelers said.

"There's only one thing to do. Start cutting," the leader of the caravan said.

"Maybe we'll come to the road they're opening," someone said hopefully.

"That's right. We can't go back, we must go on. We'd better go up this stream and follow that Indian trail."

The men began slashing trees. Wagons, livestock, women and children followed the men who went ahead to open the road. Their tools were axes, saws, and shovels. Back and forth across the river, as the Indian trail directed, they went. At times, wagons had to be unloaded, and the boxes had to be taken off the wheels to lift them over or under obstructions that couldn't be cleared away.

One day they came to an area where woodsmen had been working. Thereafter, the immigrants were able to follow a rough road until they reached the summit of the pass, where they came upon a small prairie. It was an area where a forest fire had leveled the timber until the fire had been stopped by a sheer rocky, perpendicular cliff. Further progress for that day was impossible. Men began to explore the surrounding country while others made camp. One of the explorers discovered a path to the bottom of the cliff.

"We can all get down the cliff if we have enough rope to let the wagons down over it. There's a road below."

The immigrants had learned to use ropes to guide wagons down the steep roads of the Blue Mountains, but they didn't have enough rope to reach the bottom of the precipice they now faced.

"We can slaughter a steer or two and cut their hides into strips to make a rope," a woman said.

"We can eat the steers, and there're roots and berries growing around here," another woman said. She threw herself on the ground and stretched out. "Us women need a rest, anyway. May as well take it easy, I say, while the men get those wagons to the bottom."

With cow hides supplementing the rope, thirty wagons were lowered down over the cliff. The wheel of one wagon came off, and the wagon, with its load of supplies, went crashing down the side of the precipice until it smashed to pieces in a deep canyon below.

The women, children, and livestock were able to reach the bottom over the narrow, winding trail. The caravan continued on the partly finished road down the western side of the mountains. Even though they were exhausted and their supplies of food were gone, they were happy. They knew they were very near their destination.

People in Tumwater were surprised when two strangers rode into the settlement to announce that a large wagon train had just come through Naches pass.

"We've run out of food and need help badly," one said.

At once packhorses were loaded with food donated by townsfolk. The agricultural company sent beef and a supply of flour. It wasn't long after the food arrived that 150 people sat down to a dinner of boiled beef, vegetables, hot biscuits, and coffee. A few days later those same people and twenty-nine covered wagons rolled into Tumwater.

Through the cooperative work of pioneers, Indians, and immigrants, a road had been built across the Cascade Mountains. Tumwater became the western terminus of the Oregon Trail.

# Chapter Eighteen

# Treaties

Difficult problems faced the new governor. Foremost in the mind of many white citizens was the question of legal ownership of land. There was an abundance of land west of the Mississippi, certainly ample for those who occupied it. However, white people settling in the new territories could do nothing legally with their claims until the Indians ceded land to the United States government. The determiners of policy in the government decided that parcels of land should be reserved for the Indian citizens with the land that remained available for white settlers. Attempts were made to force the Indians to adopt the white man's culture. Indeed, stipulations in the treaties, formulated by white men, constrained the red man to adjust to the ways of the whites. The red man was to live peacefully on reservations, alcoholic beverages were excluded from reservations, slaves were to be freed, and trade with the long-time merchant, the Hudson's Bay Company was prohibited.

Governor Stevens undertook the complicated task of negotiating treaties with the Indian landowners. To snarl the matter further, Governor Stevens knew little about Indians, their modes of life, their aspirations, fears, and beliefs. He called upon Mike Simmons to help him. Simmons was popular with red men. He'd mastered many Indian tongues, so communication with natives was facilitated. Simmons was appointed Indian agent for the Puget Sound area. Simmons, in turn, named Dr. Maynard Indian agent for the Duwamish Confederacy.

Although for over a year considerable effort had been expended gathering facts about the Indians of the Pacific Northwest, scant information was available to the governor and his associates about the emotional currents and superstitions of the Indians. In drawing up the specific terms of treaties, Indian leaders weren't consulted. Governor Stevens believed he'd be dealing with ignorant natives. He'd been told the Indian chiefs would readily affix a cross, signifying approval for their people, to whatever piece of paper was prepared.

When the first treaty was ready, a number of tribes were notified to meet for a council near Medicine Creek, not far from the McAllister home. Nine tribes were represented. Most of the Indians affected by the Medicine Creek Treaty belonged to the Nisqually and Puyallup tribes, numbering possibly a thousand individuals. Seven of the tribes had less than 150 members. It should be stated, however, that Indians far outnumbered whites. The census of the Territory of Washington, completed about the time of Governor Stevens' arrival, showed the white population of the entire territory to be just under four thousand men, women, and children. From data gathered for Governor Stevens, the Indians in Washington Territory numbered almost 22,000.

When the governor and his party arrived at the Medicine Creek council grounds on December 24, 1854, there were about 600 or 700 Indians present. The governor's party passed food to those present and tried to entertain them, but the Indians distrusted the governor. The second day, the governor presented gifts to all who'd assembled—small pieces of calico, pieces of ribbon, straw hats, whistles, and other objects. Although attracted to the gifts, the Indians were unhappy. They'd heard many different rumors. One, that the white people intended to send them to the land of darkness, their name for Alaska. Another rumor was that if they signed the treaty, they could take farms like the white men were taking them. After a great deal of explanation and discussion during a three-day period, some chiefs gave their consent to the treaty terms and put an "X" on the document.

Chief Leschi of the Nisqually tribe hadn't been consulted about treaty terms although he was a capable man who could've counseled the governor and his staff. When he heard the terms of the treaty, he raised vigorous objection. He said that he did not intend to give up all he and his tribesmen possessed and take several hundred tribesmen to live on 1,280 acres of land that couldn't be cultivated, had no water, and had no pasture land for stock.

Leschi and his brother Quiemuth cultivated a large acreage of bottomland in the rich Puyallup River valley. They had substantial buildings on their farms. They had large herds of horses on neighboring prairie land. Leschi was also a hunter and trapper who'd dealt with the Hudson's Bay Company for many years.

Leschi was a powerful orator. He made an impassioned speech to the assembled tribes. He said his people wanted in exchange for their homeland, bottomland to farm and prairie land for pasture. "We want low land on the banks of a river so we can paddle down stream to the fishing grounds."

Governor Stevens was aghast at the turn of events. Backed by the great chief in the nation's capital, as he so emphatically pointed out, the governor had expected childlike submission. "The treaties are ready for signatures. You Nisquallies and Puyallups have been allotted the high land above the river."

Leschi informed the governor he'd lead his tribes in battle before he'd give up tribal lands for the reservation assigned them, land on which they'd starve.

"I'll revoke the commission the government has given you," the governor replied, angered.

Leschi took the paper from his pocket, a document appointing him a chief of the Nisqually tribe, tore it up, and left the council grounds. He went back to his home and stayed for the balance of the winter. When the weather warmed, he left his home for months. People became very uneasy when they heard reports that Leschi was on the warpath, urging tribes to fight rather than sign treaties so unfair to them.

Governor Stevens was greatly disturbed. He sensed his high-handed manner had antagonized a leader whom he would've preferred as a friend. Yet it's questionable whether the governor appreciated the ramifications of the enmity he'd incurred. Leschi had been prepared to give up vast acreage, but he'd expected to retain sufficient land to support his people. The land reserved for his people was completely inappropriate.

Realizing for the first time that he'd have to be more diplomatic, the governor began negotiating the second treaty. He asked Chief Seattle to assemble the tribes of the northern end of Puget Sound for a preliminary meeting. The Indians and interested whites were to meet at a place on the waterfront near the Maynard store.

Seattle cooperated with the governor. "My tribes, Pat Kanim's tribes, and chiefs and members of other tribes will be there when your boat arrives from Olympia."

On the appointed day, the bay was covered with canoes and the shore swarmed with natives. When the governor stepped from the boat, he was given a tremendous ovation. Dr. Maynard made a short speech, then introduced the governor, who carefully explained to the Indians that the great chief in Washington wanted to buy their lands. He told them that the United States government would pay money for some of their land, but would leave many lands for reservations on which the government would build homes for them and provide them with blankets and other white man's goods. The government would build schools for their children and would send white medicine men to live on their lands to care for their sick.

He closed his speech by inviting those assembled to meet on January 12, 1855, at the camping grounds near Muckleteo for the signing of the treaties. "We'll hold a big potlatch and we'll take several days to explain, in detail, the treaty terms. An interpreter will be designated for each tribe present. We wish each person to have a chance to ask questions and to understand. Between now and the date of the signing, talk with your chiefs and your tribesmen about these matters."

Next, Dr. Maynard introduced Chief Seattle, who, he said, would speak for the Indian tribes.

Chief Seattle was accustomed to speaking to his own people. The white men assembled were his friends. When he rose to speak, he glanced toward Dr. Henry Smith. Dr. Smith nodded and moved a paper he held in his hand. Seattle smiled when he saw the paper, for he knew that the speech he'd deliver in the Duwamish language would be translated into other dialects so that all assembled could know what he said.

Dr. Smith described the Chief of the Confederation of Indian Tribes of the Whulge:

> Old Chief Seattle was the largest Indian I ever saw, and by far the noblest looking. He stood nearly six feet in his moccasins, and was broad-shouldered, deep chested, and finely proportioned. His eyes were large, intelligent, expressive and friendly in repose, and faithfully mirrored the varying moods of the great soul that looked through them.
>
> When rising to speak in counsel or tendering advice, all eyes were turned upon him, and deep-toned, sonorous and eloquent sentences flowed from his lips like the ceaseless thunder of cataracts flowing from exhaustless fountains; his magnificent bearing was as noble as that of the most civilized military chieftain in command of the forces of the continent.
>
> Neither his eloquence, his dignity, nor his grace were acquired. They were as native to his manhood as are needles and cones to a great pine tree.
>
> His influence was marvelous. He might have been an emperor, but all his instincts were democratic and he ruled his subjects with kindness and paternal benignity.[2]

---

[2] *Seattle Sunday Star*, October 29, 1887

When Dr. Maynard introduced him, Chief Seattle placed one hand on Governor Stevens's head, pointed with the other hand toward the heavens, and began his speech.

*Yonder sky that has wept tears of compassion upon our fathers for centuries untold, and that, which to us looks eternal, may change. Today it is fair; tomorrow it may be overcast with clouds.*

*My words are like the stars that never set. What Seattle says the Great Chief at Washington can rely upon with as much certainty as our paleface brothers can rely upon the return of the seasons.*

*The son of the White Chief says his father sends us greetings of friendship and good will. This is kind of him, for we know he has little need of our friendship in return because his people are many. They are like the grass that covers the vast prairies, while my people are few; they resemble the scattering trees of a storm-swept plain.*

*The great, and I presume, good White Chief, sends us word that he wants to buy our lands but is willing to allow us to reserve enough land to live on comfortably. This indeed appears generous, for the Red Man no longer has rights that he need respect, and the offer may be wise, also, for we are no longer in need of a great country.*

*There was a time when our people covered the whole land as the waves of a wind-ruffled sea covers its shell-paved floor, but that time has long since passed away with the greatness of tribes now almost forgotten. I will not dwell on nor mourn over our untimely decay, nor reproach my paleface brothers with hastening it, for we, too, may have been somewhat to blame.*

*Youth is impulsive. When our young men grow angry at some real or imaginary wrong, and disfigure*

95

*their faces with black paint, their hearts also are disfigured and turn black, and then they are often cruel and relentless and know no bounds, and our old men are unable to restrain them.*

*Thus it has ever been. Thus it was when the white man first began to push our forefathers westward. But let us hope that the hostilities between the Red Man and his paleface brother may never return. We would have everything to lose and nothing to gain.*

*It is true that revenge by young braves is considered gain, even at the cost of their own lives, but old men who stay at home in times of war, and mothers who have sons to lose, know better.*

*Our good father at Washington, for I presume he is now our father as well as yours, since King George has moved his boundaries farther north, our great and good father, I say, sends us word that if we do as he desires he will protect us.*

*His brave warriors will be to us a bristling wall of strength, and his great ships of war will fill our harbors so that our ancient enemies far to the northward, the Sinsiams, Hydas and Tsimpsians—will no longer frighten our women and old men. Then he will be our father and we his children.*

*But can that ever be? Your God is not our God! Your God loves your people and hates mine! He folds His strong arms lovingly around the white man and leads him as a father leads his infant son, but He has forsaken His red children, if they are really His. Our God, the Great Spirit, seems, also, to have forsaken us. Your God makes your people wax strong every day. Soon they will fill all the land.*

*My people are ebbing away like a fast-receding tide that will never flow again. The white man's God cannot love His red children or he would protect them. We seem to be orphans who can look nowhere for help.*

*How, then, can we become brothers? How can your God become our God and renew our prosperity and awaken in us dreams of returning greatness?*

*Your God seems to us to be partial. He came to the white man. We never saw Him, never heard His voice. He gave the white man laws, but had no word for His red children, whose teeming millions once filled this vast continent as the stars fill the firmament.*

*No. We are two distinct races, and must ever remain so, with separate origins and separate destinies. There is little in common between us.*

*To us the ashes of our ancestors are sacred and their final resting place is hallowed ground, while you wander far from the graves of your ancestors and, seemingly, without regret.*

*Your religion was written on tablets of stone by the iron finger of an angry God, lest you might forget it. The Red Man could never comprehend nor remember it.*

*Our religion is the traditions of our ancestors, the dreams of our old men, given to them in the solemn hours of night by the Great Spirit, and the visions of our Sachems, and is written in the hearts of our people.*

*Your dead cease to love you and the land of their nativity as soon as they pass the portals of the tomb— they wander far away beyond the stars, are soon forgotten and never return.*

*Our dead never forget this beautiful world that gave them being. They still love its winding rivers, its great mountains and its sequestered vales, and they ever yearn in tenderest affection over the lonely-hearted living, and often return to visit, guide and comfort them.*

*Day and night cannot dwell together. The Red Man has ever fled the approach of the white man, as the* changing mist on the mountainside flees before the blazing sun.

However, your proposition seems a just one, and I think that my people will accept it and will retire to the reservation you offer them. Then we will dwell apart in peace, for the words of the Great White Chief seem to be the voice of Nature speaking to my people out of the thick darkness, that is fast gathering around them like a dense fog floating inward from a midnight sea.

It matters little where we pass the remnant of our days. They are not many. The Indian's night promises to be dark. No bright star hovers above his horizon. Sad-voiced winds moan in the distance. Some grim Fate of our race is on the Red Man's trail, and wherever he goes he will still hear the sure approaching footsteps of his fell destroyer and prepare to solidly meet his doom, as does the wounded doe that hears the approaching footsteps of the hunter.

A few more moons, a few more winters—and not one of all the mighty hosts that once filled this broad land and that now roam in fragmentary bands through these vast solitudes or lived in happy homes, protected by the Great Spirit, will remain to weep over the graves of a people once as powerful and as hopeful as your own!

But why should I repine? Why should I murmur at the fate of my people? Tribes are made up of individuals and are no better than they. Men come and go like the waves of the sea. A tear, a tamanamus, a dirge and they are gone from our longing eyes forever. It is the order of Nature. Even the white man, whose God walked and talked with him as friend to friend, is not exempt from the common destiny. We may be brothers, after all. We will see.

We will ponder your proposition and when we decide we will tell you. But should we accept it, I here *and now make this the first condition, that we will not be denied the privilege, without molestation, of visiting at will the graves of our ancestors, friends and children.*

*Every part of this country is sacred to my people. Every hillside, every valley, every plain and grove has been hallowed by some fond memory or some sad experience of my tribe. Even the rocks, which seem to lie dumb as they swelter in the sun along the silent seashore in solemn grandeur thrill with memories of past events connected with the lives of my people.*

*The very dust under your feet responds more lovingly to our footsteps than to yours, because it is the ashes of our ancestors, and our bare feet are conscious of the sympathetic touch, for the soil is rich with the life of our kindred.*

*The noble braves, fond mothers, glad happy-hearted maidens, and even the little children, who lived and rejoiced here for a brief season, and whose very names are now forgotten, still love these somber solitudes and their deep fastness which, at eventide, grow shadowy with the presence of dusky spirits.*

*And when the last Red Man shall have perished from the earth and his memory among the white men shall have become a myth, these shores will swarm with the invisible dead of my tribe. And when your children's children shall think themselves alone in the fields, the store, the shop, upon the highway, or in the silence of the pathless woods, they will not be alone. In all the earth there is no place dedicated to solitude.*

*At night, when the streets of your cities and villages will be silent and you think them deserted, they will throng with the returning hosts that once filled and still love this beautiful land.*

> *The white man will never be alone. Let him be just and deal kindly with my people, for the dead are not powerless.*
>
> *Dead, did I say? There is no death. Only a change of worlds.*[3]

The silence that followed the conclusion of the address was prolonged and vast. It was a subdued governor who repeated the invitation to meet for the signing of the Point Elliott treaty. He suggested that the intervening time be used in discussion between tribes and among members of each tribe. He realized, too, that he should enlist the counsel and help of Indian leaders, especially Chief Seattle, in planning the potlatch and other activities at Muckleteo so that they'd be less foreign to the ways of Indians.

When the appointed time neared, thousands of men, women, and children gathered at the campgrounds. Many members of the Duwamish, Suquamish, Snoqualmie, Skagit, and other tribes arrived in a large flotilla of canoes. Other members came on foot from forest and plain. They were greased, painted, and dressed in festive attire. Some women wore skirts woven from dog hair and cedar bark. Shell jewelry adorned their necks and ankles and bits of brightly colored cloth and ribbon draped their bodies. Other women, however, were dressed in colorful dresses, second-hand costumes from England that had been acquired in exchange for furs.

A happy, expectant group greeted the governor when his boat arrived at the campground. He and the members of his party were escorted to a place of honor. The red men then sat in a semi-circle on the ground in front of the governor. Chiefs sat in the front row, subchiefs in the rows behind the chiefs.

---

[3] Rich, John M. *Chief Seattle's Unanswered Challenge*, Seattle: Pigott Printing Company, 1932.

Various tribesmen sat in groups behind their leaders. Squaws and children watched from afar.

As at the previous meeting, Dr. Maynard introduced the governor, who told the Indians that the chief in Washington was like a father who wanted his children to have food, clothing and land where they could raise crops. He told them the father in Washington knew that some of his white children would build mills, sail in ships, till the soil. He knew red men would hunt and fish and gather berries.

"We will put our names on pieces of paper, and I will send the paper to the chief in Washington," the governor said. If he says it is good, it'll be good forever."

Each chief in turn made a speech, and so ended the first day.

The second day was devoted to the festivities of a potlatch. There were ceremonial dances, sports, and gift giving. The governor's assistants dispensed gifts similar to those distributed at Medicine Creek. Women received pieces of cloth and ribbon. Straw hats, whistles, and other small articles were distributed to the men.

Chief Seattle presented a white flag to the governor. "This is a token of friendship. We'll keep our promises to our white brothers."

After accepting the white flag, the governor boarded his ship and a salute was fired. The Indians returned to their tribal lands to await the ratification of the treaty, which was proclaimed some four years later, ratification having been delayed due to the Indian wars in Washington Territory.

The governor later crossed the Cascade Mountains to present treaties to tribes as far east as the Rocky Mountains. When all were signed, the United States government had acquired legal title to over one hundred thousand square miles of territory. The Indians had received promises of reservations with homes and with schools for their children, and vague promises of blankets, clothing, and other white man's goods.

# Chapter Nineteen

# Port Madison Reservation

Chiefs' Seattle and Pat Kanim understood the meaning of the treaties they signed. Both chiefs knew it'd be futile to fight the United States government. Therefore, they bargained to the best of their ability for their tribesmen. In spite of the time and care taken to explain the provisions of the treaties, many chiefs failed to understand the implications of the documents they signed with an "X" on a piece of paper.

Land owned by a tribe was community property. Red men understood little about personal property. They didn't realize when they ceded the land to the government it'd become the property of individuals. They did not foresee that they wouldn't be able to go to many of their usual haunts for fish, game, and berries. When they began to realize what changes would have to be made in their way of life, discontent rapidly increased. Then, too, the Indians received no money and none of the promised goods due to the delays in ratifying treaties.

War started east of the Cascades. Chief Seattle wished to cooperate with the government, but what could he do? He became alarmed when some of his spies told him that hostile Indians had come through the Naches Pass and were camping on Duwamish territory.

"I fear the ancient enemies of my people are coming through the mountains to arouse my people," Seattle said.

"Oh, I don't think so," Dr. Maynard said. "I go among your tribesmen and I know they are loyal to you. I've heard the Klickitats have come through the mountains to fish."

"To fish, they say? No, doctor, you are mistaken. A few Klickitats come at times to fish; but the Klickitats are a Yakima tribe, and Yakima tribes are horse Indians, not fishermen.

"I received a report that one hundred fifty Yakimas are fishing along the White River. That is too many fishermen. Will you deliver a message for me? You see Mr. Denny often, don't you?"

"Sure I see him often, and I'll give him a message. But I don't think Arthur 'll know much about fishermen on the White River."

"Pat Kanim will, and he'll explain the significance of so many Klickitats to Mr. Denny. Ask both of them when you see them, how many hostile Indians they estimate are along the White River. Tell them I am worried."

"I'll find out all I can for you, but I think those Indians across the mountains get awful sick of wild game. All they have to do to get a change of diet is to get through the Cascades. I think they're fishing for salmon while their women pick blueberries and huckleberries on mountain meadows. I don't think we need worry at all."

The chief was not as optimistic as was the doctor. "Those Klickitats have war spirits," he thought. I don't want any of those war spirits near my people while Yakima tribes change their diet. I have to stop them. But how? There's only one way I can be sure of controlling my tribes, and that is to keep them away from hostile foes. I must move all my people to the reservation the government has allotted us. But how? One thing I can do. I can encourage the Duwamish tribesmen to move across the Whulge to the reservation."

The chief had no trouble filling Old-Man-House, which accommodated several hundred people. Chiefs and subchiefs moved there at once. Certain apartments in the building were assigned to them, their families, and followers. People occupying the building were not only protected from rainy cold weather, they were also guarded should hostile warriors invade. Four of the apartments were armed.

Old-Man-House was filled by the latter part of September. Other Indians, however, didn't want to move in September to cold, wet, temporary winter quarters.

Seattle was a man of action. "I must cross the Whulge to see the doctor. He's the Indian agent. We have to have help from the big tyee in Washington."

Going to the water's edge, Seattle ordered Indians to paddle a large canoe across the Sound to Maynard's store. The chief and the doctor talked for some time.

"You're sure the Indians don't have enough furs to keep warm this winter?" the doctor said.

"I'm sure. My tribesmen expected blankets from the government, so they traded many of their furs for metal, guns, and tobacco. The Klickitats are coming through the mountains to make trouble, I'm sure. All of my people should be moved to Suquamish territory, to the land of my ancestors. Winter will come soon with cold and snow. My people must have the blankets the government promised them when the treaty was signed."

"Your families need the blankets, even if they did trade furs for goods they wanted. The best thing for us to do is to go to Olympia to see Mike. As government Indian agent for the whole territory, he should help us."

"My men will paddle the canoe to Olympia."

But Michael Simmons, Indian agent, could do nothing. "We can't give money to help you. The papers haven't come from Washington yet. It may be months before we can get any money or goods."

"Aren't there any funds available for establishing Indians on reservations?" The doctor said.

"None at all."

Seattle was decidedly discouraged by the outcome of the trip to Olympia. "Of late, my thoughts have been black as moonless night. I feel I have failed my tribesmen. Many are sick, most have little food for winter. In the name of my tribes, I signed away our rich lands, our fishing spots, our vast forests. My people must be moved to our reservation. The Duwamish wish not to move to Suquamish land. As their leader, should I force them to leave the haunts of their ancestors? My mind does not give the answer."

"Chief, you mustn't think such dire thoughts," the doctor said. "You are a wise chief. You're good to all your people. We'll work this out somehow. Let's go put the proposition up to Meigs. He'll help us."

The Indians paddled the canoe back to Port Madison. Meigs, owner of the mill, was disturbed when he learned there were no funds available for moving Duwamish Indians to the land allotted them by the treaty.

"The big chief in Washington hasn't signed the treaty. No money yet, no goods yet," Seattle said. He told Meigs about the hostility of the Yakima tribes and about the current danger of war on the Whulge.

Meigs had great respect for the Indian chief who'd organized the Duwamish Federation of Indians, respect for the chief who controlled his own tribes, but most of all he liked the chief whom he regarded as a friend. He didn't want war on Puget Sound. He knew the best way to avert a war was to help the powerful chief, a chief who'd worked so persistently for peace.

Meigs, Maynard, and Seattle discussed the advisability of moving the Duwamish tribes to Suquamish land. The three men agreed that under the circumstances it would be best to build large community houses. Meigs agreed to cut at once large timbers, planks, and shakes, and deliver them to the reservation. The chief agreed to furnish labor, saying the Indians could build their own houses.

Maynard agreed to advance the money to pay for the labor cost of cutting the lumber. "I'm the Indian agent for the government. Later I'll collect the money I advance. We'll be able to move the Duwamish to their reservation."

While Meigs cut and delivered the lumber, the chief and the doctor worked. Both had great organizing ability. Working together, they exerted a powerful influence. Maynard took over the management of erecting the large plank community houses. Seattle sent strong young men from various tribes to assist Suquamish Indians, who, as soon as the lumber was delivered, began building the new homes.

Seattle contacted his subchiefs and urged them to move their tribes to the reservation as soon as possible. The Indians were impressed and pleased when Seattle told them the government had appointed the white doctor a Duwamish subchief and that the doctor would come to live on the reservation. Chief Seattle urged his tribesmen to move. Many of them tore down their houses, loaded their hand-hewn planks and woven mats into canoes, and moved across the Whulge. Along the shell-paved shore, they rebuilt their homes. However, many Duwamish tribesmen did not want to leave the land on which their ancestors had lived for generations, the land where loved ones were buried. The chief didn't force them to move across the Whulge. He awaited a more advantageous moment.

When the plank houses were completed, Dr. Maynard secured a sloop to be used in the moving process. The Duwamish tribesmen were invited to meet in front of Maynard's store to hear Chief Seattle speak. Fifteen hundred men, women, and children accepted the invitation. The natives listened intently to Chief Seattle.

Seattle told his people there were Indian wars east of the mountains and that hostile Indians were crossing the mountains. "I know the Duwamish don't want war. King George has moved his boundaries across the water to a big island. We're American Indians now, while the Haidas, the Tlingits, the Tsimshian are King George Indians. We need fear them no longer. Our government will protect us.

"Our big chief in Washington doesn't want us to fight each other. Nor does he want us to wage war on our white brothers. We must obey our big chief in Washington."

The tribesmen looked at each other and nodded.

"Many of our chiefs are living in Tsu-Suc-Cub. Some of our tribesmen have built houses along the shore nearby. Large houses have been built on our new reservation for you."

The Indians again began talking to each other. Seattle raised his hands. Everyone became quiet.

"We've ceded our land to the United States and they've allotted part of it to white men. We do not care if white men cut down the countless giants of the forests. We want our white brothers to build mills and homes and stores. We want their ships to sail into our harbor to bring goods to white tribes who have shown us a better way to live. We are Americans—one big tribe. King George's tribes have moved their boundaries." The chief held up his hand and pointed north.

"The Duwamish Confederacy is now part of the United States of America. Our big chief lives far away in Washington where he counsels with subchiefs. The land of my ancestors has been set aside for the Duwamish Confederacy of Tribes. I, Chief of the Suquamish tribe, welcome you to this land of ours where we can build homes, till the soil, beach canoes. We can fish in the waters of the Whulge and in its tributaries. We can paddle our canoes to the ocean to spear the whale and otter.

"We can go up streams that pass through vast lands of mountain foothills. Our women can dig roots and pick berries. We can hunt for bears or for the countless herds of elk and deer, for cougars, and other animals of the forest. We can trap beavers. When we have many furs we can work like our white brothers in woods and mills, or load ships to earn clothes and food and tools. We can all move to Suquamish land now. Our plank houses are finished."

Seattle raised his hand and pointed to the sloop in the harbor. "We have a new white subchief, your medicine man. He's ready to help us, so load your hiyu goods, your women and children on that ship. Load your light goods and your dogs in canoes. Go now. Get ready to move. Move everything you own."

"Hyak, hyak, hyak," came a voice from the clouds.

The excited Indians milled around each other, talking and gesticulating. Then they responded to the voice calling, "Hurry, hurry, hurry," and swarmed along the beach to locate the spots where they'd left their canoes.

Early in November, the loaded sloop crossed Puget Sound. Back and forth across the Sound Indians paddled canoes piled high with their belongings. The sloop made a second crossing, loaded again with women, children, the old and sick. They were cared for by Catherine, Dr. Maynard's wife, and by Angeline, the chief's youngest daughter. The two women, about the same age, had formed a friendship that lasted as long as they lived. During the hard days that followed they worked side-by-side until January first. Chief Seattle's tribesmen moved across Puget Sound to live in Old-Man-House or in plank community houses or in dwellings built on the bank above the shell-paved beach.

Moving in such large numbers was a festive event in the lives of the Indians. Getting established in winter quarters had been hard work, but the Indians were satisfied. Women of the tribe began at once to dig clams. The men knew that later they'd have to establish new beaver traps and likely go into the unexplored Olympic Mountains to hunt. They knew they'd have to paddle their large canoes into the Strait to spear the whale and the otter. It took bravery and hard work to hunt in an unexplored wilderness infested with wild animals. It took work and skill to beach a whale. The Indians were brave. They were happy to talk about the exploits ahead.

White people in the village of Seattle were relieved when they saw the Indians move across the Sound.

# Chapter Twenty

## War Clouds

•

In the years immediately following the signing of the treaties there was mounting discontent throughout Washington Territory. Indians saw more and more of the land of their ancestors taken by whites. Ceremonial and burial grounds were being plowed and planted. Fishermen found themselves denied access to their best fishing holes. Hunters were told to move on, that they were trespassing when they attempted to set their traps in the accustomed places.

Unable to procure food in the usual way, squaws and children were complaining of hunger. More and more families became destitute. Hardship was accompanied by bitterness—bitterness at a government that had failed to fulfill treaty conditions, yet expected the Indian to abide by the treaty terms.

"Like the mighty waves of the ocean, whites are enveloping us and washing us away. We die of their sicknesses. Their God, who is now our God, seems to favor white men, for He spares them and their children while our loved ones perish," was the frequent complaint.

Other causes for distress, discussed again and again by Indians, included ways white men capitalized by using Indian labor. "I work all day carrying wood on my shoulders. I walk back and forth many miles. I get tired. A white settler pays me a bag of potatoes. Does white man work all day for a small bag of potatoes? How can I feed my squaw and children? The white man isn't fair to his red brother."

"White men live strangely. He doesn't work for his tribe, he works for himself. We give white man salmon from the sea and meat of deer and cougar from the forests. He doesn't give us the potatoes and wheat he grows. He doesn't give us bread. When we take, he punishes, says we steal. White man has strange ways."

"White squaws not let us go into cabins. They say we are dirty, bring lice. They aren't friends with us. They run from us."

"Our squaws want white squaws' clothes. They want us to work like white men. Squaws chatter that white men work for their squaws. The white man is busy from first light of day until all is darkness. We don't want to always be busy. We do not want white man's ways."

Since dissatisfied Indians east of the Cascade Mountains were attacking parties of white people bound for California and the Oregon Territory, the government deemed it necessary to send troops west. The settlers organized themselves into units to help the troops should defensive action be required.

The Indians feared attacks by white soldiers. "Why bring soldiers to our land if not to vanquish us in battle and drive us away to the land of darkness?"

People in Olympia became worried when they heard that Leschi was traveling from tribe to tribe advising chiefs to pay no attention to the treaties. Residents of the "Lumber Metropolis of the West," however, paid little attention to Leschi's activities.

Chief Seattle continued to be troubled by the number of Klickitats in the woods. Seattle's scouts reported that Leschi was visiting Pat Kanim.

"Why is he visiting Pat?" Seattle said. "Leschi and Pat have been enemies many times in the past."

At the moment, however, Leschi and Pat Kanim were not at war with each other. Leschi wanted to know what Pat thought of the treaties and of the present plight of his tribesmen. He felt the best way to get Pat's viewpoint was to visit him.

The Indians of the Whulge had a caste system, so Chief Pat Kanim received Leschi with the courtesies due a chief. He and Pat talked for long hours. Pat was somewhat content with the treaties, for he believed that eventually his tribes would be moved to a reservation he regarded as suitable. Pat Kanim advised his long-time enemy to abide by the terms of the Medicine Creek Treaty.

"Bostons have a big chief in Washington. We'd have to fight many Bostons. We'd be hopelessly overpowered. Bostons come fast, like sand." Pat took up a handful of sand and let it run through his fingers.

Leschi hadn't expected help from Pat. He and Pat had never cooperated in any venture. Leschi thought, "I must go to see Seattle. I know he won't allow his tribes to make war against his white friends, but I must see him."

It was generally known that Leschi conferred frequently with his older friend, so no one was surprised when one evening he beached his canoe and entered Tsu-Suc-Cub. Seattle and Leschi talked until dawn, but could not agree.

"You mustn't go to war against the chief in Washington even if our skies seem overcast with clouds," Seattle said. "I know many of the treaties are unfair. The Medicine Creek Treaty is decidedly unfair to Nisqually, Puyallup, and Muckleshoot tribes, but do not fight. Use peaceful means to secure a better and bigger reservation for your people."

"I can't take the chance of trying peaceful ways. My tribesmen are starving, cold, troubled," Leschi said. "The Puyallup, the Muckleshoots, and the Nisqually tribes must fight against the whites. Now is the time, when many Klickitats are camping in the woods west of the mountains. If we can get them to join us in war, we can get back the lands that are rightfully ours."

"White people are many, like grass on the prairie. Indians have waged war so often they're like the broken trees on a storm-swept plain. You can't go to war against the big tyee in Washington. Your warriors would be killed or they'd have to hide in the forest like beasts. We're all Americans. We must obey our great white chief, who is our friend."

"He isn't the friend of the Indian. He's sent soldiers to help white man kill us."

"He isn't going to make war on us. He has sent soldiers to protect people traveling on the Oregon Trail and to protect people who have settled on our shores. The great chief knows that if Indians go to war against each other or against their white brothers, cruelty will prevail. You and I are chiefs. We must protect our own people. Maynard is the white medicine man of my tribe. He sets broken bones, pulls aching teeth, eases pain. My people trust him. Meigs helped my people settle on our reservation. I could not see the doctor nor Meigs tortured and killed. You have white friends, too. You've known Dr. Tolmie since you were a young boy and you have your new friend, McAllister. You could not kill your white friends."

"McAllister is not my friend. He has joined the troops to fight against us."

"McAllister has joined the troops to help keep peace on our Whulge. Go back to your farm, Leschi, and I will get powerful chiefs to go with me to see the white subchief Stevens when he returns to Olympia. We will beg him to give Nisqually a better reservation, one where you can till the soil and raise your horses." The chief, who seldom showed emotion, put his arm around his younger friend. "I can remember when you got your first horse, Leschi. Go back to your farm and wait for a fair, peaceful settlement."

"Fair, you say. Many promises have been made. The paper you signed is worthless. It is false. Many days have passed, yet the Indians have received none of the promised goods. I must fight for the rights of my people. Never will we move to that gravelly hillside to starve and die."

Thus, in complete disagreement, the two friends parted.

When he learned that his neighbor and friend, McAllister, had joined the Eaton Rangers, Leschi was puzzled. Red men and white men had lived together peacefully for many months. Leschi suspected McAllister of treachery.

McAllister had built his home on Nisqually council grounds. He and his family had many Nisqually friends. They learned to travel unnoticed in the woods. They learned to procure and preserve food from the sea and the forest. Their neighbors always had been kind, helpful, and peaceful. Great friendships developed between white children and their Indian playmates and between older members of both races.

McAllister was made a first lieutenant in the Eaton Rangers, a commission he accepted (as Seattle had judged) to help keep peace on the Whulge.

People in Olympia breathed a sigh of relief when Lieutenant McAllister reported to Eaton, captain of the rangers, that the Nisqually chiefs were on their farms. "They're repairing fences and buildings and rounding up their horses."

Shortly after the brothers, Leschi and Quiemuth, began plowing land preparatory to putting in a crop, they received word that the Eaton Rangers were on their way from Olympia to ask Leschi to sign a statement that he wouldn't go to war against pioneers in the Washington Territory, that he would give himself up to be held as a hostage so that the government could be sure he'd keep his word.

Leschi at once left his plow in the furrow, his horses on the range. He jumped on a horse and escaped into the forest. His brother followed him. The brothers went to join the Klickitats who were camping in the foothills of the mountains.

When the rangers arrived at Leschi's farm, they were unable to locate the men they sought. Instead, the rangers found the families of the brothers hiding in the woods. After sending them back to their homes, the rangers waited a few hours. Then, when Leschi did not return, they followed him into the wilderness where it was reported hostile tribesmen were camping.

"I want permission, captain, to go unarmed into the forest to find Leschi," Lieutenant McAllister said. "We're good friends and I would like to talk with him alone. You know Stali, who guided us to the farm, is Leschi's half-brother. If we go unarmed, I'm sure Stali can find him."

Mrs. McAllister became alarmed at the mounting activity on the Nisqually council grounds. Indians, faces sullen and painted black, were dancing and yelling in increasing crescendo. Understanding the meaning of war-related behaviors, Mrs. McAllister sent her oldest child, George, to tell his father about what was happening on the Nisqually council grounds. George overtook the rangers just as his father and Stali were about to start in pursuit of Leschi. George offered to accompany his father.

"No, stay with us, Captain Eaton said. "But I'll send another unarmed ranger with your father and Stali."

The three men selected had not gone far when Lieutenant McAllister was killed. The other ranger was wounded, but escaped only to be killed a few minutes later in a second ambush.

When, later, the soldiers found the two bodies, McAllister's body was hidden under a tree, carefully covered with foliage. The ranger's body had been scalped and horribly mutilated.

George McAllister approached Captain Eaton. "I must go to my mother at once. When the word of my father's death reaches Nisqually, the natives will go on the warpath against all whites. My family will be attacked and my mother is alone with my sisters and brothers."

"You mustn't try such a thing," the captain said. "You'd be shot. These woods are full of unseen enemies."

"You can't see the enemies. I've been trained by Nisqually Indians to travel unseen. That's the reason I can get through to my family. I hear signals now. I must go. Any minute I'm going to disappear. You won't be able to find me. Don't try." The youth disappeared into some underbrush.

The rangers continued their sorrowful journey to Seattle.

Using expert woodsmanship, George arrived safely to rescue his mother and his younger brothers and sisters from the mob that had gathered about his home. He herded them into an abandoned wagon, hitched oxen to it, and, following an isolated road, reached safety within the walls of Fort Nisqually.

Word of the death of James McAllister and of the continued warlike activities of Leschi reached Chief Seattle. He was fearful his lifelong enemies would massacre the white people and then cross the Whulge to make war on his tribesmen. To complicate matters even further, Seattle had found Klickitat scouts on his reservation. Then he received a message from Leschi. "If you do not join our cause, you will be killed."

Seattle discounted the message for he knew his tribesmen would protect their chief. The message indicated to Seattle that Leschi was actively preparing for war against the whites. A second message from Leschi was even more alarming to Seattle. "The Klickitats intend to kill Tyee Maynard." Seattle sent a scout to the doctor asking him to come to Tsu-Suc-Cub.

"Sick are you?" Maynard said when he arrived at the chief's apartment.

"Not sick, just worried sick. Come in."

Seattle then confided in Dr. Maynard his worst fears. "What's happening to Leschi's usually sound judgement? Even though he leads all the Klickitats and his own tribes, he'll be defeated in battle. He'll become an outlaw, forever running and hiding. From the white man's point of view, Leschi is a highly successful man. He's built up a large farm; he raises large crops; his people do not want for food; he has many horses. I am troubled. When last I talked with Leschi, I could not persuade him to work for peace. Little good is accomplished in war. Only sorrow will come to him and to his tribesmen. I weep for Leschi and for those who follow him. Now I have received word that your life may be in danger because you are tyee of the white people. You are in real danger. You must become an Indian."

"Me, an Indian? I can't imagine it, but I'll try to be one, if it's necessary."

When the doctor's disguise was completed, he walked along the beach past the chief.

"Take your glasses off," Seattle said. "Everyone knows you. No one else on the Whulge has a glass on his eye."

Since the doctor was without fear, he wore the disguise for only a part of a day. The chief became alarmed when the doctor sent word that he was in Seattle, that he planned to stay there for several days.

"Fearless is the doctor. He does not know the Klickitat tribes will try to kill tyee of white men before they start war on the Whulge. I must do something at once," Seattle said.

Seattle paddled a canoe across the water to Meigs' mill. He located Meigs near a new blockhouse that had been erected to safeguard the families of men who worked in the mill.

"Want to take a look at our new blockhouse?" Meigs said.

The two men went inside the building.

"Mighty good view from here, Meigs said. Look through those portholes. You get a view of the whole Sound. Those enemies of yours will think twice before they cross the waters to attack us. I'll tell you something that no one else knows yet. I've ordered a howitzer and ammunition. I intend to mount the big gun in the blockhouse to safeguard the mill and Old-Man-House. I'm going to give you some ammunition when it gets here."

The chief bowed his head. "Thank you," he said stoically.

The chief was 73 years old. He was tortured with arthritis. His people were destitute. They were afraid to go on the Whulge to fish, afraid of attack by hostile tribes lurking in the woods back of Seattle. They had no ammunition with which to hunt. They used bows and arrows to kill game needed for food.

The chief glanced around. "I'm opposed to war and there's no cause for war on the Whulge. But if cause for fighting comes, I will fight day and night. I thank you for ammunition to defend Tsu-Suc-Cub."

Chief Seattle told Meigs of his fear for the safety of Maynard. "The doctor went to his store. He hasn't come back."

"The doctor's all right. In the first place, there's no cause for war on Puget Sound, as you say. In the second place, the doctor has many friends. No one in Seattle would harm him. Say, I've got an idea. I'm going to Seattle right away to see about some freight on a boat probably anchored at Yesler's mill. Come with me. You can locate the doctor while I take care of my business. We'll cross the Sound in my boat. We'll circle around that ship of war to get a better look at it, then head for Seattle. Can you leave the reservation for a day to go with me?"

Meigs had no idea of the joy in the heart of the lonely old Indian chief. Stoically, Seattle said, "I can leave. I will go."

Upon arriving in Seattle, the two men went directly to Yesler's mill where they learned Maynard was actively engaged in supervising some logging, directing the unloading of merchandise for his store, and was available to anyone in case of illness. Meigs tended to the business connected with the shipload of merchandise that had arrived. Then Yesler, Meigs, and the chief went to dinner at Yesler's cookhouse, where they were served a white man's meal, an ordinary experience for the two white men, but a great treat for an Indian chief who was as hungry as his people. The chief and his tribe had ceded to the government thousands of acres of land covered with a wealth of timber, the value of which could not be estimated, land for which the government had not paid a cent even though the Indians who had owned the land were destitute.

The doctor greeted the chief with a wave of the hand when the chief passed the store on his way to visit Tecumseh and other subchiefs who were camping nearby. The reports Chief Seattle received from Tecumseh and John Kanim, brother of Pat Kanim, were most disturbing. Seattle learned there were hundreds of Indians camping between the town and the pass through the mountains. He learned that Leschi was with them.

Chief Seattle realized he must return to the reservation as soon as Meigs was ready to leave. He walked back to the business section of the settlement, where he saw a great deal of excitement. Some marines from the warship were landing on the beach, a boat had just tied up at the dock. People in the town were running toward the dock from every direction. Lieutenant Slaughter, a young graduate of West Point, was coming ashore with a company of sixty armed men.

Chief Seattle watched the soldiers march along the street. He looked at the war sloop in the harbor. His face showed no sign of emotion as he stood at attention until the marching soldiers and marines entered the cookhouse. Then the troubled chief walked to the dock and boarded Meigs' boat. He thought, "These are sad, sad times. I must be with my people."

# Chapter Twenty-One

# The Battle of Seattle

Lieutenant Slaughter received a warm welcome in Seattle. The inhabitants of the town, who'd always felt secure, knew they were doubly protected when the armed soldiers started east toward the mountains. The lieutenant and his party had gone only a short distance when the governor at Olympia received word that Pat Kanim and his warriors were following the armed soldiers. The governor immediately ordered the captain of the *Decatur* to arrest Pat Kanim and his brothers. However, the captain decided to notify Arthur Denny of the governor's order before he arrested so influential a chief.

"Pat Kanim and members of his tribe are following Lieutenant Slaughter. I must arrest him and his brothers at once," the captain said.

"There is some mistake," Denny said. "I talked with Pat when he and several of his hunters left for the Stilliguamish River on a hunting expedition. They're nowhere near the lieutenant's party. We must not take Pat into custody. We've enemies enough without arresting our friends. I promise you if you'll not disturb the Snoqualmie chief, I'll be responsible for him. I'll prove there is no truth to the rumor by going to Pat's camp. I'll bring him in."

"Don't leave town. It's not safe. Send for Pat Kanim," the captain said.

Pat Kanim not only answered the summons himself, he was accompanied by his hunters and the women and children of his tribe. He also brought along a supply of mutton and venison, with hides and horns, to prove he'd been on a hunting expedition. He took some of the fresh meat, some hides and horns to the warship and presented them to the captain. "Like my revered friend, Chief Seattle, I, my brothers, and my

119

tribesmen will not fight our white brothers who have come to live on our shores. Like Chief Seattle, we value your friendship and protection."

To have as a peaceful ally the powerful Snoqualmie chief gave the captain a crumb of comfort during the anxious days. He relayed to the governor an account of the visit of the Snoqualmie chief.

In the meantime, Lieutenant Slaughter and his soldiers proceeded toward the mountain pass. It was raining. The underbrush was wet. Weary from traveling over the muddy road, they took shelter in some buildings of an abandoned homestead. The lieutenant with some of his men went into the cabin, where they built a fire.

Just when the warmth of the fire began to permeate the room, one of the soldiers entered. "Indians are near. We can hear owl-like hoots. You'd better bank that fire. It illuminates the room too much."

A volley of shots was heard. Lieutenant Slaughter and two of his men were killed. The spray of bullets hit several others. When the volunteers placed the wounded and the bodies of the dead on litters to carry them back to the town, they could hear the victorious howls of the Indians.

After the death of the lieutenant, scouts were sent into the woods, but the Indians were so cautious little could be learned about their movements. However, a Duwamish subchief who'd been visiting hunters entered the cookhouse in search of Henry Yesler.

After listening to the report, Yesler relayed to the captain of the *Decatur* that a large number of warriors were waiting in ambush behind the town of Seattle.

A similar report reached Chief Seattle. One of his scouts reported that the Nisqually, Muckleshoots, and Puyallups had joined the Klickitats of the Yakima tribes and that Leschi was in command of many warriors who were hiding behind the trees and underbrush that surrounded the town.

Seattle wanted not only to protect white people, he wanted also to protect his own tribesmen. "There's only one way to stop war on the Whulge." Looking across the water at the *Decatur*, he muttered, "I must somehow get a message to the captain of that sloop."

He sat perfectly still for several minutes, then strolled along the beach to Dr. Maynard's home. He knew the doctor had gone to the mill to care for an injured worker, so he hadn't expected to find him at home. The chief wanted to see Princess Angeline, who much of the time stayed with Catherine Maynard. The chief remained in the Maynard home for a short while, then walked back along the beach to a pile of driftwood where he sat to watch the restless Indians. He saw Angeline and another woman come out of the doctor's home and enter one of the nearby plank houses. Later Indian women came out carrying clam baskets.

The chief watched them launch a large canoe, but apparently paid little attention to them. Angeline, with eight paddlers, could handle any type of canoe skillfully. The women paddled to a nearby clam beach, where they dug a few clams. Then they started across the water toward a distant clam beach. The sea was choppy. There was so much driftwood, it was difficult to identify a canoe. Slowly, they crossed the Sound to a beach where clams were plentiful.

Some painted warriors saw them. "What is in bottom of the canoe?"

"Clams," Angeline said, terrified.

"Just old squaws digging clams," a warrior said.

Indians on the shore of the reservation watched the clam diggers beach their canoe when they returned several hours later. "Where are the clams?" one said.

"Never again will I cross Whulge to dig clams," Angeline shouted. "We saw Klickitats in war paint, and we came back fast."

"We dig clams on Suquamish beach," another woman said. "Dig no more on Duwamish land."

Angeline addressed the wary braves, again in a loud voice. "We dig clams on Suquamish beach tomorrow." She shook her arms at them. "Go to bed."

Chief Seattle saw the commotion when his daughter returned from the clam digging expedition. Later he went to the home of the doctor.

Mrs. Maynard opened the door. "The doctor hasn't returned, but he'll be back soon, I think. Do you want to come in and wait for him?"

"I will wait." The chief entered the house, but did not stay long. "Tell the doctor I will see him at sunrise."

The doctor was waiting when Seattle came out of Old-Man-House the next morning. "We have very brave women," the doctor said as the chief sat down beside him.

Angeline had claimed that Catherine Maynard, disguised as a squaw, was in the bottom of the canoe, that she was taken aboard the *Decatur* where she talked for a long time with the captain. Angeline told her father the captain of the ship wanted Catherine to remain on the ship, but that Catherine told the captain she would return to shore with Angeline, because of Angeline's skill with a canoe.

"Do you think the war ship can stop the war?" Maynard said.

The question was answered by the sound and the echo of the shattering blast of a howitzer from across the Sound.

"I fear not. The battle has started," Seattle said.

"That's only one gun. They're probably saluting some celebrity from Olympia."

"No. I hear firing from small guns."

"You have better hearing than I have."

"I have better eyes, too. I don't need a glass on my eye to see smoke signals above a tree." The sound of another shattering roar came rolling across the water.

"You're right," the doctor said. "The battle has started."

The roar of the guns could be heard for many miles. Never in their lives had the red men, heard such deafening sounds. The chief and the doctor had difficulty controlling the natives. Terrified women and children fled into the woods, while excited braves ran along the sand, shouting. The blasting of the big guns continued for two hours, then suddenly stopped.

"What's happened?" Maynard said.

"I don't know. But I do know Leschi will try to capture or sink that ship of war. He's brave and able like white man. He won't surrender."

"That's a terrifying thought."

"It is. I must talk with my people. Will you sit in front of me while I am speaking to watch for a light above that point of land?" Seattle pointed to a cliff across the Sound. "I have a signal tower there. Take off your hat if you see a moving light. I may get a message."

The surprised doctor focused on a point across the Sound while the chief spoke to his tribesmen in a calm voice. He urged them to prepare their usual meal, to continue their usual activities.

There was a quality in the chief's voice that seemed to calm his tribesmen. Men stopped shouting. Women came from their hiding places and began to prepare food for a meal. The chief sat near the doctor to watch and wait. He thought of his youth, when, as a young man, he'd led the canoe Indians in a battle against the Klickitats, the perpetual enemies of his people. He remembered hiding his warriors in the forest while his woodsmen placed a giant tree across the river. Victory in that battle had made him chief of the Duwamish Confederacy.

"I'm very old and I am tortured with arthritis, but I am Chief of the Duwamish Confederacy," Seattle said. If there is cause for us to fight, I will defend my people and Tsu-Suc-Cub until I die. But I am praying for peace for my people, peace without war."

"Well, it sounds like war, not peace," the doctor said.

The chief saw a crimson light on the clouds. "Our enemies are burning buildings. My people will notice the light in the sky.

I must be with them again. I'll have to leave it to you to watch for the signal. Pay no attention to light on clouds, but watch that tower and take off your hat if you see a single light waving above that point of land.

The chief, walking with his staff in one hand, left to mingle with his tribesmen until, at dusk, the cannonading stopped. Gradually the Indians went to bed. But the chief remained on the beach, patiently waiting for a signal. Suddenly, he rose to his feet, stood for several minutes looking intently at a distant spot. A dim light on top of a high tree flashed up and down. The chief picked up his staff and walked wearily back to Old-Man-House.

The doctor was stretched out on a platform in the chief's apartment. "Did you see the signal?"

"I got it. Leschi is retreating."

"That's good news. Now lie down and I'll give you some medicine. You must rest."

Dr. Maynard put some water in a polished clamshell and added medicine. The chief went to sleep at once. The doctor covered him with the skin of a bear.

It was dawn when the doctor opened the door to admit two white men. The men were employees from Meigs' mill, who, with other men, had crossed the Sound to defend the town. They had returned to Port Madison to report to Meigs the details of the battle. Meigs immediately sent the men to Old-Man-House with instructions to tell Chief Seattle all they knew about the battle.

Upon receiving the report that armed warriors intended to attack the town, the captain of the *Decatur* landed a cannon and sent marines ashore to guard the settlement. Receiving the second warning from Chief Seattle that an attack on the town was imminent, the captain had some marines fire a cannon shot to warn people of the impending attack, thus giving the settlers time to reach the blockhouse.

It was about breakfast time when the battle started. Women and children fled as rapidly as possible to the blockhouse, while volunteers and marines took positions behind stumps and buildings. The howitzer was aimed at a cabin, where Indians had congregated. The shell struck the building, demolishing it and splintering nearby trees. The shot was answered by whoops from the forest. Guns began firing, the smoke indicating that the attackers were in a semi-circle.

Big guns from the *Decatur* fired shells along the line of the hostile forces. The earth was torn up. Limbs of trees crashed in every direction. The attackers shot from behind the trees and stumps directly above the settlement. Marines and volunteers returned the shots from behind the buildings of the town. Above the roar of battle could be heard the battle cries of the Indians and the screaming of their women. Fighting continued for two hours, then stopped while Indians feasted on beef that squaws had roasted.

During the lull, the marines helped white women and children move from the blockhouse to greater safety aboard the *Decatur*. Volunteers rushed from behind buildings into homes to secure valuables and food.

When they noticed the activities of the inhabitants of the town, the Indians resumed shooting, although the range of their guns wasn't sufficient to do much damage. The guns from the *Decatur* answered the muskets of the invading forces by blasting along the entire line until dusk.


A weary, disillusioned Leschi watched the superior forces outmaneuver his warriors. "The whites fight with cannon, with a plentiful supply of ammunition, with trained soldiers. I had no idea the guns on the *Decatur* and the cannon on shore could be so destructive. Although I have many more warriors than the enemy, I know not how to win. The shots from our guns don't even reach our enemy. My warriors are fearless, brave because our cause is right. But in this final effort we fail. Never will the white man allow the red man to live in his accustomed way on the lands of his ancestors. The advance of the white way of life overpowers us. We must seek refuge across the mountains on Yakima lands. My mother came from the Yakima tribe. I will go there to live. Never again will I farm my lands. Never again will I raise my beautiful horses. I wish I had never seen a white face."

Leschi started his retreat across the mountains with about one hundred fifty warriors. Encumbered with the families of some of his men, he couldn't get across the mountains without starvation for his followers unless they traveled over the frozen Naches Pass. He and his people reached the foot of the pass without food or blankets. There had been some warm weather and the snow was somewhat melted, but the night was cold and the ground frozen, so they continued on through the pass without rest.

Once over the mountains, Leschi and his warriors surrendered. They were allowed freedom and protection if they'd lay down their arms and promise never again to wage war against white people. This they did.

The defeated chiefs Leschi and Quiemuth believing they could never again return to their families or their farms, asked to be taken into the Yakima tribe. The chief of the tribe said, "We will admit you to your mother's tribe if you will become slaves." This, the two brothers agreed to do.

The governor of the Washington Territory and the army officers weren't in agreement on the treatment that should be accorded the Indian warriors. The army officers thought the Indians who surrendered should be treated as prisoners of war. The governor thought they should be executed.

"Indian chiefs who fought in the Battle of Seattle are outlaws." The governor demanded that they be arrested and delivered to Fort Steilacoom to be tried for murder.

Instead of trying to arrest the Indian leaders, the army officers reported to the governor that it would be difficult to find them. "Many of them are in hiding or have returned to the Sound. It's better to let them go."

After fearing the displeasure of white settlers, Yakima chiefs then refused to shelter Leschi and Quiemuth. They ordered them to return to Nisqually lands. Leschi escaped into the forest, where, outlawed and impoverished, he hid from his enemies. The authorities in Olympia offered blankets (the Indian medium of exchange) for the capture or the scalp of an outlawed leader. Fifty blankets were offered for the capture of Leschi.

Two of Leschi's nephews knew where he was hiding. They rode some horses to his hiding place. Leschi admired the horses, put his hand on one of them just as his nephews seized him and bound him. Then the nephews delivered him to some white men, who, in turn, delivered him to Governor Stevens.

The governor and Leschi hadn't seen each other since Leschi, at Medicine Creek, had torn up his commission and left the council grounds in anger. In the meantime, the governor had become the most powerful man in the Washington Territory while the once rich and powerful Indian chief had become an outcast.

The governor, showing no signs of compassion, ordered soldiers to take Leschi to Fort Steilacoom and put him behind bars to await trial for murder.

When Quiemuth heard of the capture of Leschi, he went to the home of a white man. "Will you deliver me to Governor Stevens? I want to be tried for murder the same as my brother."

Several men accompanied Quiemuth to the governor's home in Olympia, arriving there at two in the morning. The governor escorted the men to his office and furnished them with refreshments. Then he locked the door and left to make arrangements to send Quiemuth to Fort Steilacoom before daylight. Some men entered the office through a rear door and fired a shot, and Quiemuth was mortally wounded by an assassin.

.

# Chapter Twenty-Two

# Trial for Murder

Leschi was tried for murder—specifically for the murder of a white man named Moses. On the first ballot, eight jurymen voted for conviction, four against. The jury members were directed to review the evidence and bring a unanimous verdict. Again and again ballots were cast until finally ten jury members were for conviction. Two jurymen refused to convict a man on what they believed to be the perjured testimony of a man who swore he saw Leschi shoot the fatal shot. These two jurymen knew that Leschi was no where near where Moses was shot at the time the killing took place.

Leschi was returned to the jail at Steilacoom to await a second trial. There he remained many months. The second jury returned a unanimous verdict of guilty.

Leschi was informed the judge would listen to whatever he had to say. Leschi, in English, addressed the judge somewhat as follows:

I don't see that there's any use to say more. My attorney has said all he could for me. I know little about your laws. I have supposed that killing armed men in wartime was not murder; if it was, the soldiers who killed my people were guilty of murder, too. My warriors did not keep in order like the white soldiers, but had to resort to ambush, seeking the cover of trees, logs, anything that would protect them from bullets. This was their mode of fighting, and they knew no other way.

Dr. Tolmie, King George's man, and Seattle, the wise old chief, warned me against allowing my anger to get the best of my good sense, as I could gain nothing from going to war against the United States of America. They said I would be beaten and humbled and ultimately would have to hide in the forest like a wild beast. I did not take this good advice, but nursed my tamanawis. I went to war because I believed the white man had wronged us. I did everything in my power to beat the Boston soldiers, but, for lack of numbers and supplies, I failed. I deny that I had any part in killing Moses. I did not see him before or after he was dead, but was told by one of my men he had been killed. As God sees me, this is the truth.

Leschi was sentenced to death by hanging.

Chief Seattle, accompanied by other chiefs who hadn't engaged in the Indian wars, went to Olympia to ask that Leschi be pardoned.

Dr. Tolmie pleaded for Leschi's life, saying, "I've lived near the brothers, Leschi and Quiemuth, for a quarter of a century. I speak their language and have dealt with them for years. I know them like no other man can know them—their past character, their present impulses. The two brothers would not have taken up arms had they not been driven from their homes where they were peacefully plowing land that had belonged to their people for generations."

Other leading citizens asked Governor McMullin, who had succeeded Governor Stevens, to pardon Leschi, but the new governor did not wish to interfere with the decision of the court. Also, he feared the wrath of the white men, for they'd made Leschi a symbol for their troubles with Indians.

A scaffold was erected outside the limits of Fort Steilacoom in a natural amphitheater. The audience of white men assembled to watch the hanging of the famous chief was small. Very few Indians were present. Armed guards were sent from Steilacoom to stop demonstrations, but the guards weren't needed. A newspaper accounted of the execution read somewhat as follows:

Leschi looked up at the rope, which was being suspended. He hesitated a moment, then instantly collected himself. Knowing his life was about to end, he bowed to the spectators, made the sign of the cross, and, in Chinook jargon, said:

"Ta-te-mons, ta-te-lem-mas, ta-te-ha-le-hach, tu-ul-hi-a-sist-ah." Interpreted, the prayer means, "This is the Father, this is the Son, this is the Holy Ghost; these three in one. Amen."

His arms were secured behind him. The blindfold was put in place. The rope was adjusted and the trap was sprung.


Hanging was the greatest disgrace that could come to an Indian, but Leschi showed the spectators that he could meet the ultimate disgrace stoically, with no outward display of fear.

"Our friend, Leschi, was defeated in the Battle of Seattle," Seattle said after the execution. "He was thrown in prison for a long period. He was humiliated at the trials by his white prosecutors. He was executed by hanging in the presence of white men, soldiers, and red men. Through all the disgrace he remained a leader. As best he knew how, he tried to obtain justice for his people. I have lost a good, brave friend. I am heavy with melancholy."

Maynard tried to console Chief Seattle. "I don't believe Leschi killed Moses. He was a powerful orator. He was an agitator for fairer treatment of his tribesmen. He was guilty of leading the attack on Seattle. Always he favored the British over the Americans. But I think he was innocent of the crime for which he was hung."

"Quiemuth is gone. Leschi is gone. The Nisqually and Puyallups will miss their brave chiefs. I am old, sad, sick, and weary. Soon there will be no noble chiefs left. What will happen to red men in this land that has now become the land of the whites? When white men first came to our lands, I thought there was land enough for all. Now I see that is not so.

"I loved Leschi like a son. My heart has bled during this long time he has been in jail, on trial, and awaiting execution. The feelings stirred up in settlers during these uncertain times seems to have been directed toward Leschi, yet he was only one of the attackers. If he was guilty of murder, so also were whites and other Indian leaders.

"At least we who were Leschi's friends can take some comfort from the fact that he won for all his people all he had been striving to win. The new treaty gives the Nisqually and Puyallups the rich farmland their ancestors have had for generations, land which includes the farms of Leschi and Quiemuth. Actually, his oratory and bravery won, for Leschi long will be remembered as a martyr.

"I have lived a long time and have seen much unfairness. Watching Leschi grow from childhood and prosper in early manhood, I never expected to see him fall so low. He was a peace-loving man. He abhorred cruelty, especially to animals and children. He lived peacefully side-by-side with King George's men at Fort Nisqually for many years. I suppose his best friend was Dr. Tolmie, from whom he learned many white man's ways.

"Part of his undoing was the favoritism he displayed toward King George's men. The Bostons did not like that. How strange it is that it was peace-loving Leschi who was driven to battle his white brothers. Leschi was betrayed by his own kin, a nephew he'd raised as a son. The nephew received fifty Hudson's Bay blankets. He paid for his treachery with his life, so perhaps justice was done."

"Yes. Another Nisqually hunted him and shot him for his betrayal of Leschi."

"I, who am almost eighty years old, live to mourn Leschi, who should've had many more years of life to enjoy his horses, his farm, his wives, his children and grandchildren, and his tribesmen. Life brings much happiness, but it brings much sadness, too. I weep today."

"Buck up, my good friend," the doctor said. "The wars are over. Many settlers have returned to their farms. Soon the city, which bears your name, will be a bustling metropolis once again. Red men and white men, Americans all, are living in peace."

# Chapter Twenty-Three

## Peace at Last

After the Battle of Seattle, the chief seldom left the reservation. He liked to climb to the top of a large sawdust pile. There he was warm, and from that vantagepoint he could see visions come true.

One day Tyee Maynard joined him on top of the sawdust pile, pointing to a ship coming into the harbor. "Is that the kind of ship you talk about?"

"Yes. Probably King George's ship."

"I suppose it carries the usual cargo of old clothes and scrap metal to trade for furs."

"It does and my people have furs piled in canoes ready to go out to that ship when it stops."

"It looks pretty good to see Indians wearing shirts and pants, doesn't it?"

"Shirts and pants are not enough," Seattle said. "You know some of the men who work in the mill have married Indian maidens. Indian women with their white husbands live in some of the cottages. White children and children of Indian mothers play together and attend the same school."

Both men were silent for a few minutes.

"You see a schoolhouse and a meeting house for white people," Seattle said. "Look on that hillside and you see white houses for white man's families. Now look at our reservation. No schoolhouse. Look at the huts along the beach where my tribesmen live. Our men want the white man's nails and tools. I want the white man's bread and molasses for my people. You are our friend. Can't you get our promised goods and money from the government?"

The doctor shook his head. "I've asked many times, but no goods come."

"Has the government paid you for the money you advanced when you helped us move to this reservation?"

"Not much yet, but probably it's partly my fault. I didn't know enough to send my bills through the right channels. I must tell you something funny. Once I asked the government for some flea powder and they sent almost a shipload of it. I can tell you, that flea powder did a lot of good."

The chief laughed.

"Let's get down off this sawdust pile and go to the community house where you can sit on a chair while I show you a map of the United States," Maynard said. If you'll look at it, I think I can show you why you haven't received your goods."

"Go down this way. Don't ever try to walk down a sawdust pile. Stay here while I get down first."

The chief slid gracefully down the steep incline of an enormous pile of sawdust. Maynard tried to follow. He sprawled down the incline. When he reached the bottom, the chief helped him brush the sawdust from his clothes. As the two men walked to the community house, the doctor noticed the chief leaned heavily on his cane. Upon entering the building, the chief dropped into a chair. "Have you ever seen a map of our country?" Maynard said.

"I have seen maps, yes." The chief pointed with his cane to the northwest corner of the map. "That water is our Whulge. Beyond it is water that separates us from our ancient enemies—the Haida, Tlingit, and Tsimshian." Seattle then pointed to the city of Washington. "Our big chief lives here."

"I see you understand the map. Our trouble is this. White men from the north are at war with white men in the south." The doctor pointed to the states in the northeast and then to the states in the southeast. "President Lincoln, our chief now, wants to free black men who are slaves."

Seattle looked intently at the map. "Where are the black slaves?"

"They are in the south."

Seattle examined the eastern part of the map. "Why do white men wage wars?"

"In this case, they're at war to free those black slaves. Many of those men who are fighting each other are friends."

Seattle and Maynard were silent for a minute or two.

"Black slaves must be free," Seattle said. "I gave freedom to all my slaves on Suquamish land long ago—just after I was baptized by the man in the black robe. And when big chief in Washington said that all slaves on reservations must be free, I made Duwamish tribes free their slaves. At times I used a club, but the big chief in Washington can use peaceful means to free slaves, can't he?"

"I know it's hard to understand, but men in the north are at war with men in the south. Supplies must be sent to men who are fighting. Ammunition, food, clothes must be provided. Our big chief doesn't have enough goods to send to red men all over the United States, especially to those in far away lands like ours."

Seattle looked across the room at the map of the world. "I understand. England is an old country with many ships. We are a new country with few ships. Now our chief wants to free black men who are slaves, so red men must help free all slaves. We are Americans, just like our white and black brothers, so we must help. We must hunt more, fish more, while our women and children dig clams, pick berries, dig roots for food."

"I'm sure we're going to have to wait awhile—you for your promised goods, and me for the money I advanced."

As the men left the community house, the doctor noticed again how heavily the old chief leaned on his staff. They had not gone far when they heard a voice.

"Hey, there," shouted Meigs. "I've found you at last. I've been hunting everywhere for you, Maynard. I can't go to Seattle today, but I'll leave the first thing in the morning."

"All right, anything you say."

"By the way, chief," Meigs said, "I'm going to stay in Seattle a couple of days. Would you like to take a ride across the Sound on my boat?"

"I will go," the chief said stoically. He showed no emotion, but the men knew he liked to cross the Sound to see his daughter, Angeline, who'd never moved to the reservation. She lived in an old hut on the beach. She did housework in white people's homes.

Strangers in Seattle called the Indian woman an old squaw, but the early pioneers knew her as Chief Seattle's daughter, and they called her Princess Angeline. People who lived in the largest town on Puget Sound wanted to build in their city a fitting home for a princess, but Angeline didn't want one. She preferred to continue to live in her home on the beach.

The morning after Meigs, Maynard, and Seattle crossed the bay, the doctor located the chief at the dilapidated home of the princess. "It's early, but I want to show something to you. Do you think you can walk through the woods and up a steep hill? Your cane will help you, and I'll give you a hand if you need additional help."

"I can go."

The two men trudged up a steep incline through dense woods until they reached the top where stood a massive two-story building.

Seattle looked at the pillars across the front of the building and he thought of the pillars along the front of Tsu-Suc-Cub. He thought of a great potlatch on the white sand of a beach.

"What do you think of this for a building?" asked Maynard.

Seattle studied the wide two-story building. "I think my potlatch house is still the largest building on the Whulge, and Suquamish built it without the help of oxen or whirling saws or metal tools. But I wonder about that dome. Can you tell me how a white man got it to the top of that high house?"

"I don't know. I only know it's a mighty big school house to be located in this wilderness."

136

"A school house for white children," mused the chief.

"Children won't go to school in this building. It's for young men and women. It's a college, the University of Washington."

Seattle looked bewildered. He glanced at the forests, at the mountains, gazed at the rising sun. He smiled.

"What is making you smile?" asked the doctor.

The smile on the chief's face broadened. He laughed aloud. "I have just seen a vision. You know my tribesmen are leaving the reservation to work in woods, in fields, to fish far out at sea. Soon my tribes will be lost among the masses of people who will inhabit these lands. Young men and young women who are descendents of my tribesmen will walk up these steps to learn much. What did you say is the name of this school?"

"The University of Washington."

The bell in the dome of the university rang out. The doctor noticed a surprised expression on the chief's face, saw him glance at the sky and saw his lips move slightly.

Men standing nearby stopped working. One of them said, "Did you hear the echo?"

"I guess it came from the top of that hill behind the university, but it's the first time I've ever heard it."

Another said, "It's mighty strange. I been workin' here a long time and I ain't never heard it before. That echo came from up in them clouds."

The doctor glanced at the chief's impassive face, then said, "They've not finished the inside of the building, so I guess we'd better not tackle those steps today. We'll come back again when the building is finished."

The doctor walked ahead of the chief down the steep hill. The chief returned in Meigs' boat to Suquamish land.


Chief Seattle grew weaker as the days passed. Seldom did he leave the potlatch house. It was warm near the fireplace.

There he could lie and watch the flames and think of days gone by.

One day the doctor entered. "So you're lying down, are you?" He took hold of the old man's wrist. "I've heard you're sick, so I've come to see you."

The old chief clung to the doctor's hand. "Can you give me some medicine?"

"I can, in just a minute or two."

After preparing the medicine, the doctor said, "Open your mouth now and swallow this."

The chief swallowed the medicine and went peacefully to sleep. The doctor knew the chief's life would soon end, so he called a native priest.

When the priest told Seattle he was dying, the chief nodded. "All is well with me. It is well I am going." He was silent for a minute. "Will you ask Meigs to shake my hand before I am laid to rest in the ground?"

The chief closed his eyes, never to open them again, having failed to get money for his land and help for his tribesmen.

Word of Seattle's death spread rapidly. The big mill closed for a day so that people could attend the funeral. Many canoes and boats landed on the white beach in front of Tsu-Suc-Cub. Meigs sent his boat across the Sound so that those in Seattle who had no means of transportation could attend the services.

Upon the conclusion of the funeral mass, Meigs went to the coffin. He took the chief's hand in his own and held it for a short time. Then he walked slowly back to his seat.

Indians who were standing near the coffin reported that the chief smiled. Perhaps he did, for he was far ahead of his time and race in wisdom and foresight. He knew his influence was so profound that had he gone to war during the Indian wars, all other chiefs on his Whulge would have joined him and every white person on the shores of Puget Sound would have been killed. He knew that had he sent an order from his signal tower, the mills would have been set aflame, small towns would have been burned, and the city that bore his name would have been destroyed forever.

He knew the thunder spirit was vanquished and the spirit of the sea gull prevailed when hundreds of white men and red men crossed the Whulge to be with the last Suquamish chief as he went to rest in the land of his ancestors.

# About the Author

In the fall of 1881, Ida Belle Westover received word that if she wanted to see her mother, Christina Minor Martin, alive again, she'd better return to Modale, Iowa. She was pregnant at the time, and the trip from Ord, Nebraska was difficult.

Her mother died as predicted, but winter had set in and Ida couldn't make the return trip until after the birth of the baby. Florence Christina Westover was born Christmas Day, 1881 in Modale, Iowa.

As soon as she was able, Ida Belle started back to Ord with little Florence. On the way back, the stagecoach was snowed in a few miles from Ord. Led by her husband, William Ambrose Westover and an uncle, Robert Nichols, a deputy U.S. Marshall, a rescue party came to get them.

When she was one year old, Florence's father moved the family to Seattle by immigrant train. For a time he was deputy state land commissioner, and while in Olympia, Florence endured the first tragedy of her young life, witnessing the drowning of her brother Guy. The family eventually moved to Chehalis where her father opened a law office, and, in later years, served as mayor. There she graduated from high school at sixteen, and two days after her 17th birthday she married the high school principal, Elias A. Bond.

They had five children, one of whom, Margaret, died in adolescence of pneumonia. The other four each served in the U.S. Navy during WW II, attaining the rank of Lieutenant Commander, each earning Ph.D. degrees in education. During 56 years of marriage to Elias, Florence ran a good sized chicken ranch, and, as one of the first female licensed building contractors in the state, built a number of houses.

It was during her early childhood, however, that Florence had experiences, which would influence her interest in Native American cultures and early pioneer days. She developed a relationship with a number of Indians, among them, Princess

Angeline, daughter of Chief Seattle. Florence's father, being an educated man and an attorney, had contact with many persons of note, both Indian and white. In her late teens she was quite an elocutionist, winning several medals in competition.

All of her other accomplishments and experiences notwithstanding, Florence Westover Bond was a marvelous storyteller, first enchanting her children and grandchildren by the hour. These two books, The End of the Trail (originally titled The Charm String Stories), and Chief Seattle, Man of Vision, are her legacy.

Printed in the United States
2073

9 780759 650855